V-V

DATE DUE

SEP 20 79			
JUL 17 '80			
DEC 17 19??			
JAN 23 19??			
SEP. 13 1983			

The High Rocks

Also by Loren D. Estleman:

THE HIDER
SHERLOCK HOLMES VS. DRACULA

The High Rocks

LOREN D. ESTLEMAN

DOUBLEDAY & COMPANY, INC.

GARDEN CITY, NEW YORK

1979

Library of Congress Cataloging in Publication Data

Estleman, Loren D
The high rocks.

I. Title.
PZ4.E815Hl   [PS3555.S84]   813'.5'4
ISBN: 0-385-14696-5
Library of Congress Catalog Card Number 78-62646

First Edition

To my mother and father, once again and with feeling.

The High Rocks

CHAPTER ONE

For three years running, the north central section of Montana's Bitterroot Mountain range was struck by a series of harsh winters that paralyzed transportation and left the old-timers with nothing to talk about in the way of worse winters gone by. During one ninety-day period, temperatures plummeted from a record one hundred and five degrees in late August to minus forty-two on Thanksgiving Day. Winds blasting straight down from the North Pole swept snow clouds before them in an incessant stream, smothering the jagged landscape beneath shrouds of snow which in March of the third year obliterated all but the roofs and the church steeple in Staghorn, the one settlement that had managed to survive in the ruthless climate of the Bitterroot.

Most of the damage, however, remained undiscovered until the final spring thaw, when the snows receded and landowners were able to gaze for the first time upon the winter's legacy. Cattle were found frozen stiff in huddles of up to a dozen. Barns and corncribs were crushed flat beneath tons of snow or smashed to splinters by the avalanches that heralded the onslaught of warm weather. Great trees that had stood for centuries jammed narrow mountain passes where they had fallen after being uprooted by the tremendous pressure of the glaciers sliding down from the peaks. Corn and silage, deprived of its shelter, had been taken up by the heavy winds and strewn all over the countryside,

leaving without food what little livestock remained. Everyone had his work cut out for him in the spring of that third
year.

But whatever their troubles, no matter how large a task
they had ahead of them, the people of Staghorn and its en-
virons could take comfort in knowing that there was one
who was worse off than they. Somewhere in that sprawling
wilderness, far above the level they considered safe in any
season, there existed a man who had elected to brave the
winter's perils alone and unprotected. Of all the mountaineers, he alone had not come down from the high country at the first sign of blizzard. And when the flood waters
had subsided and the time had come to see about gathering
together the fragments of their lives, the farmers paused in
the midst of rebuilding their barns and laying new sod on
the roofs of their houses to look up at the hostile mountains and ask:

"I wonder how Bear made out?"

Bear Anderson was as much a part of the lore of that
wild region as the Flathead Indians, who still took time out
occasionally to cross the mountains in order to do battle
with the nomadic tribes over the game-rich plains that
flanked the foothills, or the marauding packs of wolves that
terrorized farmer and cattleman alike when the snows were
deep and game scarce. To children he was the Bogey Man,
a figure of towering menace who would swoop down from
the mountains and devour them at a gulp if they neglected
their chores or failed to say their prayers before retiring.
The name given to him by the Indians was unprintable in
any language, but in moments of charity they called him
Mountain That Walks, a force more to be avoided than
reckoned with. To everyone he was a presence, a thing sel-
dom seen but nonetheless there, like the great pines that

grew high on the snow-capped peaks and were seen close up only by mountain goats and soaring eagles.

He was the son of a Norwegian logger and his Swedish wife who had come there early in the 1830s, lured by tales of virgin timber and the riches that awaited the man who could carry his weight in the lumber camps. Those who had known Thor Anderson said that he was nearly six and a half feet tall and capable of felling a white pine in fifteen fewer strokes than it took his closest rival. His wife, Greta, bore him six sons, four of whom died in infancy. Of the fifth, Olaf, little was known except that he marched off to fight for the Union in 1861 and never returned. That left Bear.

If that was his true Christian name, or if it had been bestowed upon him because of his size, no one knew. Bear he had always been, and Bear he would always be. It was a name that suited him like the sun the sky. Of the two surviving sons, it was he who most took after his father, both in build and disposition. At the age of twelve he was six-foot-two and still growing; by his twenty-first birthday it was said that he had surpassed his father, with arms like pork barrels and shoulders so broad he had to swivel them to get through a doorway, like a deliveryman carrying a kitchen stove. There was no denying that at his maturity he was the biggest man in Staghorn. That he grew to be larger than his father could not be proved, however, because by that time Thor Anderson was dead, and so was his wife, Greta.

In the 1860s the Bitterroot range served as a buffer zone between no fewer than four Indian nations. To the northwest lived the Kootenays, avid hunters who nevertheless avoided tracking game into the mountains for fear of coming into contact with their mortal enemies, the fierce

Blackfeet who made their home along the upper Missouri
River. Eastward lay the territory of the Crows, the boundaries of which remained fluid as they moved with the migra-
tory bison, a year-round source of food, clothing, shelter
and fuel. In the mountains themselves existed the Flatheads, or Salish. Of all the savage tribes, these were the most
feared, as they were known to cross the mountains in
search of a fight, and it mattered little whether their victims were Crows or white settlers, for they lived only to
spill blood. Long periods of uneasy peace laced with spo-
radic outbursts of violence had made the prospect of living
in the mountains an unsettling one for all but the Flatheads. It was only by a cautiously maintained system of
trade and tribute that any white was allowed to remain
above the level of the plains, and there were times when
even that was not enough, as the Andersons learned early
in 1862.

The War Between the States was not a year old when
Bear returned from an overnight hunting trip into the
mountains, a buck deer slung across his saddle, and discovered his parents' cabin burned to the ground. The snow
that had not melted before the heat of the blaze was trampled with moccasin prints and the tracks of unshod horses.
Inside, he found his parents—what was left of them—
huddled together beneath the charred debris of the bed-
room as if Thor with his last act had tried to shield his wife
from the Indians' attack. Near the bodies lay the double-
bitted axe which Bear had seen his father use every day of
his life; the blade was clotted with blood and hair, singed
and blackened by the fire. That meant that one brave at
least had paid for this slaughter, probably with his life.
There was not a scrap of food or a usable good to be found
anywhere in the wreckage of the cabin, and the horses
were missing from the lean-to stable out back. The motive

for the slayings, then, was clear; the Andersons had been guilty of having more than the savages.

It took a fire almost as large as that which had consumed the cabin to thaw out the ground enough for Bear to bury his mother and father. When that was finished he left and, according to all acounts, never returned to the site. He took along only his horse, the supplies he had with him, and his gun, a Spencer carbine. There was nothing else to take.

That, at least, was how the people of Staghorn put it together from the evidence and from the tales told by the occasional friendly Blackfoot who came to town to trade for meat and corn. He was not heard from for months, and then only secondhand, in the pidgin English of those same Indians. The story they had to tell spread swiftly throughout the settlement and provided the basis for the legend that was to come. Mountain That Walks, they reported, had begun to take Flathead scalps.

His first victim was a boy less than sixteen years old. Armed with only a knife, the youth had been sent alone into the wilderness as part of the traditional test of manhood. His failure to return to camp at the end of the allotted period prompted a search, at which time his corpse was discovered lying wedged between two boulders at the bottom of a steep ravine. At first the braves thought he'd fallen, but upon climbing down they found that his throat had been cut and his hair lifted. Nearby they came across the boy's knife, thick with blood. He had been killed with his own weapon.

Infuriated, Two Sisters, the Flathead chief, dispatched a party of braves to track down and apprehend the killer. They never returned. After three days a second party was sent out to find out what had happened to them; they came back with the corpses draped over the backs of their

horses. Every member of the original group had been shot
and scalped. The dead braves were buried in full state,
after which, upon the advice of the medicine man, no more
parties were sent out.

That had been fifteen years ago, and in the time between then and the end of that third deadly winter Bear
Anderson had not been seen more than a dozen times, and
then only for a few minutes at a stretch by the Indians
with whom he traded. Each time, they swore, he had fresh
scalps swinging from his belt. The trade completed, he
would depart, vanishing among the tall stands of pine toward no one knew where. How he knew that the Flatheads
had been responsible for his parents' deaths remained uncertain, but most believed that he had followed the telltale
tracks from the burned-out cabin to the Flathead camp. In
any case, they were the only Indians he killed.

More than once he had been thought dead. But each
spring brought new tales down from the high country, tales
of raids on small Flathead encampments and warriors following tracks that led nowhere. It was said that in some
camps the women appealed to the Great Spirit to rid them
of this evil shade that struck and vanished, only to strike
again many miles away within minutes. And the squaws
were not alone in their concern. At night the mountaineers
would sometimes look up and see reflected in the low-hang-
ing clouds the fires of great war councils convened for the
sole purpose of plotting one man's destruction. Their plots
bore no fruit; he remained as elusive as the spirit the
women believed him to be.

But this time it was different. The three successive winters that had lashed the Montana section of the Great Di-
vide had been the worst in the territory's history. If wild
game could not survive them—and there was plenty of evidence, once the snow was gone and the forests began to

stink of death, that much of it had not—what chance stood a man? As the weeks crept by, and spring hardened into summer with no sign in the settlement of the beautifully cured furs that Bear used for trade with the non-Flathead savages who remained friendly to him, it became apparent that at last the legend had met its master. Conversations around cracker barrels swung slowly away from the subject of the scalp-hunter to the new administration in Washington and the market price of grain. It was at about this time that Staghorn's complacency was shattered by the most sensational story yet to come down from the lofty peaks.

When the story came to be told, it was appropriate that it was White Mane who told it. A tall brave whose sinew had long since shriveled to dry flesh stretched over bare bone, this Blackfoot was well past the age at which his fellows were usually abandoned by tribal custom to the Indians' death spirit. It was believed that he was allowed to live only because his stubborn independence prevented him from becoming a burden to the rest of his tribe. Once a year he came down out of the mountains, laden with furs from animals he had trapped and skinned, to bargain with Bart Goddard at the mercantile for whiskey. Although it was against the law, Bart always gave him what he wanted in return for the pelts, partly out of greed and partly because he knew that the old man drank the whiskey himself and kept it hidden from the young braves in whose systems the spirits were as dangerous as a fire in a dynamite shack. Besides, White Mane was a consummate storyteller when his tongue was loosened by strong drink, and nobody loved a good tale more than Bart Goddard.

It seemed that three weeks previously, the old warrior had been on his way to the river to check his traps when he stumbled across a scene of carnage such as he hadn't witnessed since the last war with the Flathead nation.

Flathead braves lay about the glen in every position, most of them shot, two stabbed, one with his throat and face slashed beyond recognition. All were missing their scalps. Near the edge of the clearing, White Mane discovered a warrior who was still breathing, despite the fact that he had been stabbed and his hair also lifted. The brave lived just long enough to tell him what had happened.

The Indians had been part of a hunting party on the trail of a grizzly one of them had wounded. When they stopped to water their horses at the river, it was discovered that four of their number were missing. Since these four had been riding at the rear of the detachment, and Mountain That Walks was known to pick off stragglers, a great deal of excitement ensued when the absent braves did not respond to calling. Like the people of Staghorn, however, the Flatheads had been of the opinion that Bear had perished during the winter, and so they were quickly mollified when the head of the party dispatched two warriors to look for the miscreants. It seemed likely that the four had found something the others had missed and were off on their own trail in pursuit of the grizzly.

When at the end of an hour the searchers had not returned, the party doubled back to find out what had gone wrong. They hadn't traveled over a mile when a sharp-eyed buck spotted something in a clearing several hundred paces to the north. The party rode in that direction—and came to an abrupt halt when they saw what that something was.

They were standing in the center of a circle of tall poles, from the tops of which dangled six bloody scalps.

The leader had barely enough time to raise a cry of retreat when the first shot rang out and he fell from his horse dead. Six more shots sounded, as fast as a rifle could be cocked and fired, and when the last one echoed over the mountaintop only two braves remained on horseback. One of them bolted for the surrounding forest. The other—he it was who told the story—watched in horror as a huge creature which he at first thought was the grizzly they had been tracking dived headlong from the branches of a nearby pine, collided with the rider, and carried him to the ground. A knife flashed, followed by a bloodcurdling scream. Then the beast rose to its feet and stood looking down at the still form which a moment before had been a hot-blooded brave with thirty scalps to his credit. It was only at that moment that the remaining Indian recognized the beast as a man.

Snatching up his rifle, the Flathead gave vent to a war cry and charged the killer. The latter looked up sharply as if he had forgotten about him, and leaped aside just as the Indian fired. The bullet missed him and shattered a limb on a nearby tree. As the brave pounded past, the man on foot reached up with one enormous hand and wrenched the rifle out of his grip. In the next instant the rifle swung around and the butt came crunching up against the Indian's temple. The Flathead felt a bursting pain in his chest as he fell. After that he remembered nothing until he awoke with his bloody head being supported by the old Blackfoot's hand. Moments later he died.

The story grew in the retelling, and by the time it reached the newspapers back East it was reported that Bear Anderson had slaughtered thirty braves with his bare hands and skinned them to make a coat. In no time at all he was a figure of national renown. Articles about him, which bore no resemblance to the facts, began to appear in newspapers from New York to Oregon. Lurid paperbound novels describing his supposed adventures filtered westward from the great publishing empires along the East Coast. In July a correspondent came to Staghorn all the way from Chicago, spent some days talking with the citizens and asking

questions, then left; two months later he published a book
in which he claimed to have spent six weeks with Bear Anderson up in the Bitterroot, where the scalp-hunter related
his life story exclusively for the journalist. By the fall of
1877 Thor Anderson's boy rivaled Wild Bill Hickok and
Buffalo Bill Cody for reader interest in places where Indians were things unknown and a gun was something worn
by a policeman.

The interest was not confined to the East, however, and
that's where I come in.

CHAPTER TWO

Arthur's Castle was the somewhat exotic name for the four-story hotel that stood at the north end of Staghorn's main street, but it fit; operated by an Englishman who insisted upon being addressed as Sir Andrew Southerly, it was the only place I knew of in the Northwest where the towels were as thick as rugs and there was a bath to every floor. The fact that there was only one attendant, who could haul buckets of steaming water to only one bath at a time, was immaterial; in an area where bathtubs of any kind were scarce as passenger pigeons, the presence of four in one building was a luxury almost unheard of. They were the hotel's main attraction. If you're wondering why I bother to go into so much detail concerning bathtubs, it's merely to explain why, when first encountered in this narrative, I am naked.

I had been sent out from the U.S. marshal's office in Helena to bring back a wife-murderer named Brainard who had been picked up on a drunk and disorderly charge in Staghorn, where the sheriff had identified him from his description on a wanted dodger. Now, it was a rule of Judge Harlan Blackthorne's court that each of his deputies check in with the local peace officer immediately upon reaching his destination, but it was a rule of my own not to let any rules hinder me. I figured that if Brainard had waited during the week's ride it had taken me to get there, he'd wait a little longer while I freshened up at the Castle. What I

hadn't figured on was the impatience of the local peace
officer.

I was immersed to my chin in nearly scalding water
when the doorknob began to turn. My gun, a .45 caliber
Deane-Adams English five-shot revolver, was hanging in its
holster on a chair beside the tub. I palmed it and drew a
bead on the door between my bare feet, which I had
braced against the tub's cast-iron lip. I cocked it just as the
door swung inward.

The steam rising from the tub was so thick I could
barely make out the dark smudge of a man's form standing
in the doorway, but that was enough. In my profession,
when someone comes in on you without knocking first,
you've got to figure he isn't there on a friendly visit. I'd
learned that the hard way; the same thing had happened to
me twice before and two men were dead because they
hadn't taken that extra second to brush the door with their
knuckles. My finger tightened on the trigger.

"You still carrying that dandy's gun, Page?" drawled a
deep voice with a faint trace of Mississippi around the r's.

I held onto the gun. Boot Hill is full of those who put
their weapons away when they heard a voice they recognized.

"It's this way, Henry," I said. "Only two men in the
West ever carried a gun like this one. The other was Bill
Hickok. You figure it out."

He laughed then, and I knew it was going to be all
right. Even so, I didn't relax my grip on the revolver until
he came farther into the room and I could see that his gun
was safely in its holster. I let the hammer down gently and
leathered the five-shot.

Henry Goodnight hadn't changed much since I'd seen
him last, which was going on three years ago. Hatless, he
wore his auburn hair shoulder-length, the way some of
them still do up in the mountains, and he dressed like a

banker, complete with Prince Albert coat and shiny beaver-skin vest with a gold watch chain glittering across the front. The effect was somewhat marred by the silver star he had pinned to his belt. His gun was ivory-handled and rode waist-high in a cut-down holster designed to carve seconds off his draw. He had moist brown eyes, kind of gentle and slow-looking, that had fooled more than one self-styled fast draw into thinking he could take him. To date, none had. He had been elected sheriff of this isolated community of trappers, farmers and cattlemen eight years before and there had not been an election since. The locals recognized a good thing when they had one.

"You've changed some," he said, grinning behind his moustache. "Back on Ford Harper's spread you wouldn't take a bath but once a month, and then only when it rained."

I grinned back. I'd almost forgotten those days when we made our way from one cattle camp to another with one rope between us and a pair of backsides like buffalo skins. "What makes you think this isn't my first this month?"

"From the looks of the water, I'd say it was."

"There's a lot of dust between here and Helena." I extended a soapy hand, which he took in a grip usually reserved for the butt of his six-gun. "What's on your mind, Henry? You know I would have showed up at your office sooner or later."

"More likely later." He swung a black-booted foot up onto the seat of the chair and leaned forward with his forearms resting upon his thigh. This made him look casual but alert. It was one of a half-dozen or so poses he had practiced to the degree that he could go into any one of them without looking as if he were affecting it, which he was. Henry was vain as a bride. "Hobie Botts told me he saw you ride in half an hour ago. I need your help."

"Don't tell me your prisoner got away."

His teeth glittered behind the reddish fringe along his upper lip. "You know me better than that, Page. When was the last time I let a prisoner escape?"

I shrugged, soaping the back of my neck. "I haven't seen you in three years, Henry."

"I suppose I deserved that," he said. "What I've got is a drunk and disorderly over at Goddard's who's a mite more drunk than I can ignore and a damned sight more disorderly than I can tolerate. If you listen close you can hear the glass breaking clear over here. He's got friends with him who are behaving themselves, more or less, but I can't say I trust them if it comes down to me or him. The town doesn't give me a deputy. How'd you like a part-time job? Say, fifteen minutes at the outside?"

"Indian or white?"

"Half-breed. His name's Ira Longbow, and he's hell with any weapon you put in his hand. Some folks say he's the son of old Two Sisters himself, but no one knows for sure. He acts like he believes it. Can I count on you?"

I sighed. "Hand me that towel."

Dressing, I ignored the change of clothing I'd laid out and put on the outfit I'd worn during the ride from the capital, stiff with dust and sweat. I didn't want to get any blood on my fresh linen. I put on my holster without bothering to tie it down—my gun was going to be in my hand all the time anyway—and together we left the hotel and crossed the street in the direction of the mercantile, a long low building constructed of logs that served a dual purpose as general store and saloon, with a thin partition in between. Henry hadn't exaggerated; the sounds of breaking glass and splintering wood were audible all over town.

Something big fell apart with a tremendous crash as we neared the building. I winced. "Goddard won't be happy with you for taking so long to investigate."

"Bart's been acting lately like he owns me and everything else in town," he said. "It won't hurt him to be taken down a notch or two. Here he is now."

A beefy old man who had been pacing the boardwalk in front of the log building came storming over to meet us, pushing his way through a crowd of onlookers. He had thick white eyebrows and a great shock of hair of the same color which had a habit of tumbling over his forehead like an avalanche of fresh snow. It had been white as long as I'd known him, and I'd been born and raised in Staghorn. "Where the hell you been?" he demanded of the sheriff in a voice just short of a bellow. "That son-of-a-bitch breed is running me out of business!"

"Hello, Bart," I said.

He glared at me in a preoccupied manner from beneath the shelves of his eyebrows. "Page Murdock," he said. "I heard you grabbed a badge up at the capital." Without waiting for an answer, he returned his attention to my companion. "What about it, Sheriff? Are you going to do something about that maniac, or do I go get my shotgun?"

"Hold onto your hat, Bart," drawled the other. "What got him started this time?"

"How the hell should I know? I ain't no injun. He come in falling-down drunk, and I refused to serve him. That could of been it." Something struck a wall inside the building hard enough to knock the chinking loose from between a couple of logs. He jumped at the noise. "You going to stop him while I still got a place of business?"

"Where'd he get drunk, if not here?" asked Henry.

"What is this, for chrissake? Everything I own is being smashed to bits and you act like I'm the bastard that's doing it. There's a dozen families run stills up in them mountains that don't care who they sell to; why else you think I got to operate a mercantile? The competition here is worse than in Virginia City!"

The sheriff looked thoughtful. "I sure hope you're telling

the truth, Bart. I warned you last time if I ever caught you serving liquor to Indians, I'd close you down."

"You won't have to. Two more minutes and Ira Longbow'll do it for you!"

We left him fuming in the street and stepped up onto the boardwalk. The crowd parted respectfully for the dashing figure of the sheriff, taking little notice of the dusty saddle tramp at his side. My gun was in my hand. Henry's remained in his holster, but with him that was as good as holding it. With his left hand he gave the bat-wing doors on the saloon side a shove and stood back while they swung shut. When no bullets followed he cautiously led the way inside.

It was a long room with a low ceiling, half again the length of a railroad car and several feet wider, leaving less than a third of the building for the mercantile on the other side of the partition. Red- and green-striped Indian rugs decorated the bare logs that made up the walls. A number of hooded kerosene lamps swung from the ceiling. The glass had been broken out of two of them, which explained the oily tang that accompanied the normal saloon smells of cheap whiskey, stale sawdust, and sweat. Smashed tables, bottles, chairs and glasses formed a pile against the walls and bar. The big mirror on the wall behind the bar was a web of jagged cracks forking outward from a triangular hole in the center where something had struck it, giving me a fly's-eye view of the rest of the room and its contents.

A trio of youths stood behind the bar, two of them drinking quietly while a third poured himself a tumbler full of amber liquid from a brown bottle in his left hand. They wore leather vests that had never touched cactus and narrow hats with cocked brims that had never held a horse's fill of water. They dressed alike, looked alike, even wore their cartridge belts at the same low-slung level in imitation of a gunfighter in a dime novel. Kids. I treated them as I would any nest of baby rattlesnakes that blocked my way out of a cougar's lair; I kept them covered. The fourth youth was Henry's worry.

Standing in the center of the cleared section, he was a scarecrow, bones and sinew covered by skin the dusky red shade of old barn siding. Dull black hair hung in lifeless wings on either side of his forehead from the part in the middle. The whites of his eyes, though bloodshot, were dazzling against the lackluster copper of his complexion, in the centers of which the irises were as black as his hair and as shiny as the buttons on an old maid's shoes. His nose was fleshy, his lips thick and flat. Wisps of downy black beard clung like spun sugar to his cheeks and chin. His clothes were homespun and faded, his boots run down at the heels. He wore no gun belt. His hat, a black Spanish affair with a low flat crown, hung between his shoulder blades from a thong knotted at his throat.

He stood with his legs spread apart and the upper half of his body bent forward at the waist, swaying slightly, as if the weight of the Dance six-shooter he held in his left hand was slowly pulling him over onto his face. The barrel showed a tendency to drift as well, but it remained pointed in the general direction of the sheriff.

Somewhere along the line, Henry's own gun, a Colt Peacemaker with the front sight filed off and the hammer shaved to ease the trigger pull, had leaped into his right hand. I hadn't seen him draw, so he must have done it as we were entering and my attention was claimed by the three at the bar. Not that I would have seen it in any case. Eight men had died who hadn't. He covered the half-breed.

I could see that the boy with the bottle was going to go for his gun before he made a move. They get a special look on their faces when they're thinking about it, kind of sly and frightened at the same time. I fired, there was a crash, and he was holding the neck of the bottle and nothing else.

"Don't," I advised him. He took it in the right spirit. He raised his hands.

"There's two ways we can do this, Ira." Henry spoke in his professionally tough voice. "I can take you to jail and you can sober up in a cell that's not too dirty, or I can turn you over to Josh Booker. Your choice."

That meant something only to those who knew their way around Staghorn. Josh Booker was the local undertaker. If it meant anything to Ira Longbow, however, he didn't show it. He maintained his unsteady stance, his gun barrel-to-barrel with Henry Goodnight's.

I decided to toss my own two bits into the pot. "You boys had better talk some sense into your partner," I told the three at the bar. "If that Dance goes off, you're next."

"You can't shoot all of us," muttered the youth at the far end. His tone was petulant, scarcely audible, like that of a boy talking back to his mother, but who wasn't sure he wanted to be heard.

"Why not? This gun holds five cartridges, and I've only fired one. That gives me one to play with." None of them seemed to have an answer for that.

Henry took control of the conversation. "What's it going to be, Ira? I'm being paid by the month."

Ira seemed to be having trouble making up his mind. His black eyes shifted, glittering unnaturally in the light seeping in through the grimy front window past the blurred white faces pressed against the panes. "Go away, Sheriff," he said at last. His voice was pitched low for his age, muddied slightly by his condition. "This ain't your business. Me and my friends are just having some fun."

"At whose expense? Give me the gun before someone

gets hurt." Henry held out a steady left hand to receive the weapon.

The boy at the far end of the bar snatched at the butt of his gun and I shot him. The bullet struck his left shoulder just below the collarbone, spun him around, and slammed him into the cracked mirror, bringing a cascade of glittering shards showering down around him. His revolver somersaulted from his grip and glided along the polished surface of the bar until it reached the edge, from where it dropped to the plank floor with a thud. In the same instant I recocked the Deane-Adams and brought it to bear on his two companions. They threw up their hands, shaking their heads frantically. The one closest to me still held the neck of the bottle my first bullet had shattered in one hand.

The wounded youth stood with his back against the wreckage of the mirror, his right hand gripping his left shoulder, blood oozing between his fingers. His face was dead white.

"Three left," I told him, unnecessarily. His gun was beyond his reach and all the fight was gone from him.

I glanced in Henry's direction and was surprised to see that he was standing there alone. At his feet sprawled Ira Longbow, a purple bruise swelling on his left temple where the sheriff had brought the barrel of his six-shooter smashing against the half-breed's skull. The youth's gun lay two yards away where it had landed after leaving his hand. Henry wasn't paying any attention to him. He was busy sighting down the muzzle of his Peacemaker and scowling.

"Bent the barrel, damn it," he growled.

"You should've used the butt," I told him. "Indians got hard heads."

Now that the danger was past, the room began to fill with people. The sheriff showed them his gun and they backed off, leaving a clearing around the scene of destruction. He fished a shining coin from his coat pocket and tossed it to a young boy dressed in threadbare homespun, who caught it in one hand. "Go fetch Ezra Wilson," Henry directed him. "Tell him we got a wounded man here. Hurry!" The boy took off at a run, his leather worksoles clapping on bare wood.

"What happened to Doc Bernstein?" I asked.

The lawman regarded me dully for a moment, as if he'd forgotten all about me. "He's dead. A small raiding party led by Two Sisters hit his place last year and burned it to the ground. They found Doc in the front yard and skewered him with a war lance. His wife and boy were in the cabin when they put the torch to it."

"Oh."

Ezra Wilson was a gray little man whose features, once out of sight, were impossible to recall. They were crowded in the middle of a face that seemed to grow straight out of his detachable collar with no neck in between, broader at the top than at the bottom and crowned by a head of washed-out red hair parted in the middle and pomaded to the extent that it looked as if he hadn't grown it at all, just painted it on with a thick brush. He walked like a crab and carried a cylindrical black bag like a doctor's. He was Staghorn's barber.

"See what you can do for him, Ez," said Henry, indicating the young man with the hole in his shoulder.

I watched as the barber directed the youth to take a seat in one of the few unbroken chairs and removed his vest and shirt. The wound was as large as a baby's fist and glistened with blood, but no bone had been touched that I could see, there being no chips visible.

"Passed clear through," piped Ezra, reaching into his bag and withdrawing a bottle of alcohol and a roll of gauze,

items most likely appropriated from the late Doc Bernstein's effects. He proceeded to clean and dress the wound,
not too gently. The young man whimpered and bit his lip a
lot.

"Why'd you do it?" I asked the patient. I had collected
the guns from all the parties involved and heaped them on
what was left of the table in front of me.

"I recognized you suddenly." The petulance was still in
his tone, tempered by pain. His breath came in gasps. He
probably thought he was dying. I would too, after a quar-
ter of an ounce of lead had slammed through me.

"So what?"

"You're Page Murdock. Everyone says you're fast. I
wanted to see how fast."

"The hell with fast," I said. "I already had my gun out.
Anyway, Henry Goodnight's faster than I am; why didn't
you try to take him?"

"I wasn't out to commit suicide."

"So instead you collected a bullet in your shoulder."

He shrugged, then regretted it. "I'm still alive, ain't I?"

"You're damn lucky. I was aiming for your belly."

The barber finished dressing the wound and stood back,
wiping alcohol off his hands with a broad white handkerchief. "What you want done with him now?" he asked
Henry.

The sheriff looked at me. "You pressing charges?"

"If I do, does it mean I have to stick around for the
trial?"

"You know it does. You're wearing a badge. Carrying
one, anyway," he corrected, noticing that I wasn't sporting
one of the tin targets Judge Blackthorne handed out.

"Forget it," I said. "Chalk it up to high spirits and let
him go. Without his gun, of course."

"Of course." There was a sneer in Henry's tone.

"You might as well turn the others loose too, if you've a mind. They haven't done anything but watch anyway."

The lawman holstered his damaged weapon. Taking this as a cue, the two youths who had emerged unscathed from the shoot-out helped their wounded companion to his feet and left, supporting him between them.

"You'll get paid, Ezra," Henry told Wilson. "I know the boy's parents."

Bart Goddard came loping into the room, head down, barrel torso tilted forward, nearly bowling over the barber, who was on his way out. The face beneath the mop of dry white hair was crimson. He took in the damage with a sweeping glance. "Who's gonna pay for all this?" he demanded.

Henry shrugged. The fate of his six-shooter had put him in a sour mood. "You'll have to talk to Ira about that after he sobers up." He caught my eye. "Give me a hand getting him over to the jail."

That wasn't as easy as it sounded. The half-breed couldn't have weighed over a hundred and twenty, but it was all dead weight and raising him to his feet was the most physical labor I'd engaged in for some time. When at last we had him supported between us, Goddard glowered at him from beneath the heavy mantel of his brows.

"There ain't enough wampum in this old man's whole tribe to take care of what he done today," he said.

Henry said something to him that for reasons of delicacy I will leave out of this narrative, and together we trundled our burden across the street to the jail.

The warmth put out by the little iron stove hissing away in a corner of the sheriff's office was a welcome change from the damp chill of the street. It was still September, and already the first icy blasts of winter were making their presence felt at that high altitude. Old-timers whose sole purpose in life was to predict the weather were laying odds that the region was in for yet another severe winter, perhaps the harshest yet.

The jailhouse was the second that had been built on that spot since Staghorn's founding fifty years before. The first, a log affair with a sod roof and no foundation, had perished within two years of its construction when a prisoner set fire to his mattress during an escape attempt and the flames spread to the walls, eventually engulfing the entire structure and killing the arsonist. In its place rose a stone building with steel bars on the windows and thick wooden shutters with gun ports in the centers which could be swung shut and locked in the event of a siege from outside. The office, a rectangular enclosure separated from the four cells in back by a flyblown wall, was furnished with two straight chairs and a desk with a scaly finish created by too many layers of cheap varnish. Its top was a litter of dog-eared wanted circulars and telegram blanks, many of which were soiled with coffee rings. A chipped enamel coffee pot, once white, now blackened at the base and up one side, gurgled insistently atop the stove and boiled over, its contents sizzling upon the iron stove top. The smell this made was harsher than burning hides but not as acrid as spent gunpowder. In any case, it was not an appetizing aroma.

We went through a thick oaken door at the back of the office and deposited Ira Longbow in the cell nearest the door. The one opposite was already occupied. I studied the face and form of the man stretched out on the cot through the bars and checked them against the description on the wanted circular I'd been carrying in my hip pocket. Short, squat, black hair thinning, prominent jaw, incongruous button of a nose permanently reddened by a lifetime spent chugging cheap whiskey. Pointed ears. Mean little eyes.

Forearms as big around as my calves. It was a perfect match. Leslie Brainard, the Helena teamster who had strangled his wife to death in an argument over money.

"That him?" asked Henry.

I nodded. "I'll grab a good night's rest over at the Castle and pick him up in the morning. I've earned that much."

"Just so you get him the hell out of my jail. He's the most unaccommodating prisoner I've ever had."

"What's this situation with the Flatheads?" I asked him, when the connecting door was shut and we were back in the office.

He unbuckled his gun belt and draped it over a wooden peg beside the front door. "It's Bear Anderson again," he said. "Every time he takes a scalp, Two Sisters uses it as an excuse to go on another raid. Usually he confines himself to horse-thieving and looting. Doc Bernstein and his family were the first white casualties in years. It's coming to a head fast. The army's trying to get the Flatheads to sign a treaty, but they aren't going to get anywhere as long as Anderson's still up there."

"Which means they won't ever," I said.

Henry eyed me curiously. "You know him, don't you? I forgot."

"I grew up with him. I'll bet Bear and I explored every cave and crag in those mountains as kids. To get him down, they're going to have to find him first. Then they've got to take him. That's a job I wouldn't hand out to my worst enemy."

"Funny you should say that."

The voice wasn't Henry's. It was thin as a razor and marked by a high Ozark twang, something like a bullet ricocheting off a rock. My back was toward the front door. I turned.

The voice's owner was as thin as the voice itself, and short enough to walk under my outstretched arm without ducking. Even so, the outsized hat he wore, together with a yellow ankle-length duster, made him seem even smaller than he was. His face was ordinary except for a crossed right eye that even when it was looking straight at you appeared to be focused on something beyond your shoulder. His nose was prominent but not gross, his hair, what I could see of it beneath the broad brim of his sweat-darkened hat, the color of wet sand and long enough in back to brush his collar. Sandy whiskers, some twelve or thirteen days old, blurred the lines of his chin and emaciated cheeks.

He had two men with him, who looked enough alike and had enough years separating them to be father and son. Both wore their hair long, the old man's dirty gray compared to the younger man's brown, and their clothes, neutral in color beneath a skin of dust, were trail-worn and frayed at the cuffs, collars, knees and seats. Their eyes were small and close-set above huge hooked noses, beneath which their faces fell away to scrawny necks with hardly any chins to interrupt the sweeping lines. They were clean-shaven, or had been until about two weeks before. The young man wore steel-rimmed spectacles and had a long-barreled percussion cap pistol stuck in his belt. The old-timer carried no weapon that I could see. Saddle tramps, both of them, with just enough of a furtive look about them to be wanted for something.

"Who are you?" I asked the man in the duster.

"Name's Church." When he spoke, he had a habit of grinning quickly with all of his white, even teeth, but it was more of a nervous habit than an expression of emotion, as nothing he said seemed humorous. "These here are

Homer Strakey, Senior and Junior." He tilted his hat brim in the direction of his companions. "Which one of you is Sheriff Henry Goodnight?"

"I'm Goodnight," said Henry, cautiously. He edged nearer his six-shooter hanging on the wall. "What's your business?"

"They told us over at the saloon you got a breed name of Longbow locked up in jail. I'd like to bail him out."

"What for?"

"I need a guide. Folks around town say this Longbow knows them mountains like nobody else. What about it? I got the money."

"Mister, I wouldn't send a yellow dog up into those mountains this time of year," said Henry. "What do you want up there that won't wait till spring?"

Church unfolded a sheet of paper he'd had in a pocket of his duster and handed it to him. I read it over his shoulder. It was a warrant for Bear Anderson's arrest, and it was signed by President Ulysses S. Grant.

CHAPTER THREE

"Would you mind explaining this?" asked the sheriff, handing back the shopworn scrap of paper at the bottom of which the presidential seal was a gray smudge.

"I don't see why I got to, but if it'll spring the breed I don't suppose it'd hurt." Church refolded the warrant and returned it to his pocket. He had strong hands, callused on the insides of his thumbs and forefingers and strung with tendons as taut as telegraph wires. "Chief Two Sisters has refused to talk peace with the army till Bear Anderson is gone from the Bitterroot. General Clifton met with Grant last April to get permission to send in troops, but the President didn't want to give the injuns the idea he was making war, so he signed this here warrant and ordered Clifton to hire a civilian to do the job. Well, it so happens the general remembered the good job I done for him a couple of years back when he sent me into Canada after a bunch of deserters, so he wired me to come see him. I get twenty a week and expenses, with five thousand waiting for me when I bring in Anderson, dead or alive." His eyes slid in the Strakeys' direction. "We're splitting that, of course."

Junior giggled then, a high, keening neigh far back in his nose. The effect on me was the same as if a rat had just scrambled over the toe of my boot.

"Well, Grant's not President any more, but I suppose his signature's still good," said Henry.

"Church," I said, after a moment's reflection. "I knew

I'd heard that name before. The way the story was told to me, none of those deserters made it back to the fort alive."

The man in the duster swung his attention back to me, or so I thought. With that crossed eye it was hard to tell. "Who are you?" he demanded.

I told him. The grin fluttered across his face like bat's wings. "Hell," he said, "you're a fine one to talk. You've kilt your share."

"I'm not above killing," I said. "Back or front, it makes no difference to me, as long as it has to be done. That's where we disagree. You just kill. I don't even think you like it, particularly; you just don't feel anything about it, one way or the other. That's what scares me. You don't care."

"You're breaking my heart." He returned to business. "What about it, Sheriff? Do I get the breed or don't I?"

"In the morning. Let him sober up first." Protecting his left hand by wrapping his linen handkerchief around it, Henry lifted the coffee pot and poured a stream of steaming liquid into a yellowed china mug he had retrieved from atop the clutter on his desk. At no time had he strayed more than two steps away from the gun in his discarded holster, and he kept his right hand free; Church and his two friends made that kind of impression. "I'll talk to Bart Goddard tonight and get an estimate of the damages. If you can pay that, I guess you can have Longbow. If he doesn't object."

"We was figuring on leaving tonight." The bounty hunter's tone was mildly insistent.

"Then you're lucky he's in jail. Nobody travels in the mountains at night. Not the Flatheads, not Bear Anderson. Nobody. It's a good way to get dead."

"Why? What's up there?"

"Wolves, for one thing." Henry studied the steam rising from his mug. "There's not much game left after last winter, so they're traveling in packs of a hundred and more. They'll attack anything that moves. Also, there's a chance your horse will step in a chuckhole in the dark or lose its footing while you're feeling your way along one of those narrow ledges that wind around the mountains, and nobody'll find your body till spring. And if you get past all that, you've still got grizzlies to worry about." He leered behind his moustache. "Outside of that, it's a waltz."

Church stared at him for a moment with that peculiar detached gaze. At length he shrugged, his duster rustling with the movement. "I guess we got no choice any way you look at it," he said. "Where can we get a room for the night?"

The sheriff directed him to Arthur's Castle.

"We'll be back first thing tomorrow." Church left, followed by the younger Strakey. The old man hesitated a moment, ruminating absently on what appeared to be a plug of tobacco distorting his right cheek, but could just as well have been a rotten tooth. Then he, too, withdrew. He walked with a strange, rocking limp, putting me in mind of a trail cook I once knew whose right leg was an inch shorter than its mate. When he was out of sight, Henry took a big swallow of his scalding coffee, as if to get rid of a bad taste in his mouth.

"If that's what the army is hiring these days, I'm glad I got out while I was still a corporal," he said.

"Don't underestimate Church," I told him. "All the stories I've heard about him end the same way; he gets his man and collects his bounty."

"If he does it this time, he'll have earned it. What about those characters he has with him? Bent or not, I'd bet my six-gun they're wanted somewhere."

"That's your worry." I stepped toward the door. "Take good care of my prisoner, will you? I'd hate to have to explain to Judge Blackthorne how you managed to poison him with that coffee of yours."

"Where are you going now?"

I leered. "Charlene McGrath still in business?"

"You're too late. She pulled out for Deer Lodge last week. Won't be back till April."

"I can't wait that long." I scowled. "Guess I'll just pick up a bottle and get quietly drunk in my room."

"Make sure it stays quiet. I've got too many drunk and disorderlies locked up now." His eyes twinkled over the rim of his china mug.

I collected my key from Sir Andrew at the hotel desk and went up the carpeted stairs toward my room on the second floor. On the landing I met Church, who was on his way down. He had discarded his hat and duster and was wearing a striped shirt without a collar and a pair of pants, fuzzy at the knees, which had once belonged to a gray suit. The bone handle of what looked like a Navy Colt protruded above his holster, curved forward for a left-handed draw. His sandy hair was beginning to thin in front, a condition he attempted to conceal by combing it forward over his forehead, Napoleon-style. He stopped when he saw me.

"Me and the boys been in the saddle quite a spell," he said. "You know where we can find us some female companionship?"

I told him the sad news about Charlene McGrath. He cursed and continued on his way, leaving behind a smell of leather, sweat and dust. The bounty hunter seemed to be one customer who wasn't attracted by the Castle's many baths. He stopped at the desk, where I heard him ask Sir Andrew what any single man asks the hotel clerk his first night in a strange town. The answer he got was the same one I'd already given him, so maybe now he believed me.

I didn't sleep well that night. Maybe it was because,

after seven nights of sleeping on the ground, I couldn't get used to the acre of featherbed with which the Englishman provided each of his guests, but I didn't think so. My mind kept wandering back to the thought of Bear Anderson alone in the mountains with a bird dog like Church on his scent. That the mountain man could take care of himself was something he had proved again and again throughout the decade and a half that had elapsed since the murder of his parents, but the bounty hunter had spent at least that much time proving the same about himself. Why I cared at all was another mystery. It had been a long time since Bear and I had seen each other, and I doubted that he'd even recognize me. Growing up together didn't mean we were friends; he'd never saved my life or anything like that, nor I his, and no matter how hard I tried I was unable to remember a scrap of conversation that passed between us during all the time we spent together hunting and explor- ing in the Bitterroot. At length I gave up trying to puzzle it out and went to sleep just as false dawn was beginning to di- lute the blackness outside my window.

My first stop after rising some two hours later was the barbershop. After a shave, I went over to Goddard's mer- cantile, where I ordered supplies for the trip back to Helena from the owner's hawk-faced wife, Hilda. The prices there were twice as high as any I'd encountered dur- ing the trip across the territory. I secured a receipt from her after paying and stashed it away in my coat pocket among the others to be used as proof when I presented my list of expenses to Judge Blackthorne. Leaving the stuff there for the time being, I then went to the livery stable.

The man at the stable was new, but only in the sense that he hadn't been there on my last trip to Staghorn. He was an old jasper in a greasy slouch hat with a square yel- low pencil stuck in the band and a face like a peach pit. As

I approached he squinted up at me from his seat beside a pot-bellied stove in the livery office and rose creakily to his feet when I asked him for my horse.

After he led it out of its stall—it was a big buckskin I'd had five years, fresh from a rubdown and a night's sleep—I inquired about Leslie Brainard's horse. The old man stared at me, blinking in confusion.

"It's all right," I said, showing him my badge, which I kept in my breast pocket. "He's my prisoner."

"It ain't all right." His voice reminded me of two tree trunks rubbing together in the wind. "He ain't got no horse."

"He didn't walk from Helena," I pointed out, patiently, I thought, under the circumstances.

"Oh, he had a horse, but that was before he lost it over the poker table to a pair of treys." The old man laughed noiselessly, opening his mouth to display a toothless cavern and heaving his chest in and out like a skinny bellows. "Reckon that's what made him disorderly."

"No wonder the territory's in debt," I grumbled, and asked him to show me what horses he had for sale.

He sold me a chestnut mare that had seen its good days, but none of them since Appomattox. The saddle and bridle were twelve dollars extra. I collected a receipt for that, too, as well as for the horse and my own animal's care, knowing all the time that the judge was going to argue the validity of the dirty scrap of paper with the old man's mark at the bottom, and after returning to Goddard's and loading the supplies onto my horse's back, I led the animals over to the sheriff's office.

I found Henry seated at his desk over a mug of hot coffee which, from the smell of it, might have been the same one he'd been sipping the night before. Mingled with the burnt-grain odor was the unmistakable scent of Bay Rum.

"You've been to the barber already," I reflected.

His slow brown eyes looked me over from head to foot, taking in my clean clothes and freshly shaven face. "Look who's talking," he growled. He was one of those who aren't to be trifled with until after they've had their second swallow of coffee. "That cross-eyed son of a bitch got me up at five o'clock this morning to turn over his precious half-breed. There's nothing to do in this town at five o'clock but get a shave, and I had to get Wilson out of bed to do that. I enjoyed that part," he added, smiling maliciously.

"That explains his mood when he shaved me." I fingered the strip of gauze covering the nick at the corner of my chin. "Did Church go the damages?"

"Eventually. At first he tried to pay it off in army scrip. When I told him what he could do with that, he dug out a purse full of double eagles heavy enough to break your toe and counted out what I'd told him. I'm thinking of going into the bounty-hunting business; it pays better."

"Where's my prisoner?"

He sat staring at me until I realized what he was waiting for and drew out the warrant signed by Judge Blackthorne. When it was on his desk he left it there without glancing at it, slid open the top drawer, and handed me a ring of keys. "You want a pair of handcuffs?"

I shook my head and showed him my own, a pair I'd had forged especially for me in Butte. On the other side of the connecting door, I handed them between the bars to Brainard and told him to put them on. He glared at me murderously with his mean little eyes, but he did as directed, sliding the manacles over his huge teamster's wrists and snapping them shut with a grating noise that

made me wonder if I should have cleaned them after accidentally dropping them into the Beaverhead River last
spring.

"He got a hat and coat?" I asked Henry on the way out.

The sheriff jerked his head in the direction of the peg beside the front door, where hung a black-and-red-checked
woolen jacket with patches on the elbows and a shapeless
brown hat. I retrieved them and handed the hat to Brainard. "Put it on."

"What about the coat?" His tone was a belligerent
snarl.

"Those cuffs stay on," I told him. "If it turns cold you
can slide it over your shoulders like a cape. Maybe it'll keep
you from getting any ideas."

He pulled on his hat with a savage thrust.

I shifted my drawn gun to my left hand and offered
Henry my right. "Take care, Henry. I'll see you next trip."

He accepted it. "Keep an eye on him. He's craftier than
he looks."

"I wasn't planning on inviting him to bundle with my
sister."

We left town at a walk, headed south and east in the direction of the Clark Fork River. The air smelled of rain, or
possibly snow; there was a metallic sharpness about it that
set my facial muscles to tingling. The buckskin's breath
was visible in gray jets of vapor. Two miles out, Brainard,
riding several yards ahead of me, got out his coat and wres-
tled it onto his shoulders. By nightfall we were within sight
of the Clark Fork. The sky was overcast and leaden.

I dismounted first, then drew my gun and pointed it at
the teamster. "Off." When he was standing, I directed him
to lie on his stomach while I removed my horse's saddle.
He did so, cursing when he scraped the side of his face
against a bull thistle and squirming to get away from it.

There's something about making a stupid mistake that, no matter how it finally turns out, haunts you for the rest of your life. Since that moment I've come up with a dozen ways to handle the same situation without risk, and I've used just about all of them. That day I didn't.

I was undoing the cinch of my saddle when the buckskin shrugged its powerful shoulders. The buckle shot out of my hand and the saddle slithered away from me and fell to the ground on the other side, blanket and all. I muttered a curse and ducked under the horse's belly to retrieve it. In that moment my prisoner hurtled to his feet and brained me with a rock he'd picked up from where he'd been lying. I swam to the ground through a red swirl.

CHAPTER FOUR

Either it was dark when I awoke or I was blind; for a long time I wasn't sure which was the case. I was lying on my back where I'd fallen, which meant that I'd turned over or had been turned over by someone else. That was convenient, as I was able to turn my head and retch without drowning myself. Not that it made me feel any better. At the bottom of the hill, the rush and gurgle of the river competed with the pounding inside my skull, and the pounding won. I wanted desperately to slip back into unconsciousness, to experience sweet oblivion, but at the same time I sensed that if I did I would never come out. With a superhuman effort I heaved myself up onto my knees and staggered to my feet. Twice I nearly fell, but at last I managed to place a steadying hand against a slightly yielding surface that turned out to be the flank of the chestnut, which was busy munching at the tall grass that carpeted the slope, and got rid of what was left in my stomach. That left me feeling more human, but just a little.

Gingerly, I raised a hand to the back of my head—and took it away as if I'd touched a hot stove. There was a soft spot the size of a half dollar beneath the damp and matted hair. A little more effort on Brainard's part, and I wouldn't have gotten up at all.

My gun belt was, of course, missing, as was the key to the handcuffs. I took advantage of the light cast by the three-quarter moon to search for the cuffs themselves and found them a little farther down the slope with the key still in the lock. My horse was gone as well, which spoke well for the teamster's taste, along with my saddle and the saddlebags filled with supplies. I found my hat where I'd fallen and put it on, tilting it to avoid the injured area, then mounted the mare on the second try and turned it in the direction of town.

It couldn't have taken me longer if I'd crawled the distance. Long before the mare's hoofs struck the washboardlike surface of Main Street, the sun, a pale glow behind the cloud cover, had floated clear of the distant peaks and the streets had begun to fill with early-morning shoppers and merchants on their way to roll up the blinds in their windows. Snowflakes the size of wood shavings danced and swirled about in the air. It wasn't cold enough for them to stick, however, and so they vanished as soon as they touched the ground.

I dismounted before the sheriff's office, nearly folding when my weight came down on my legs, and caught Henry just as he was locking up before going over to the Castle for breakfast. Today he was wearing his hat, charcoal gray with a low crown, a wide, sweeping brim, and set off by a gold band—the style of headgear favored by gamblers who preferred not to store their derringers in plain sight. The brim wasn't wide enough to conceal his look of surprise when he saw me swaying before him.

"I need a fresh horse and supplies," I told him. "Get them for me, will you, Henry?" Then I fell into a heap at his feet.

The room in which I came around smelled strongly of carbolic and something else almost as pungent. Summoning all my strength, I forced open my eyelids, which evidently someone had sewn shut. Ezra Wilson's gourd-shaped face swam into focus, dissolved, then came back and stayed. I noticed that the pomade had begun to lose its grip on his hair, allowing a band of pink scalp to peep between the loosened locks near his crown. His starched collar, missing now, had left its mark in the form of two horizontal red welts at his throat. His features seemed even more pinched than normal. Beyond his head, a water-stain shaped like a buzzard with a broken wing adorned the yellowing plaster of the ceiling.

The mattress beneath me was not one of Sir Andrew's featherbeds. A little thicker than a poorly constructed quilt, it was stuffed with straw and studded with metal buttons that dug into my back like pebbles. I could feel the slats beneath it. There were four of them running sideways, not enough to support my one hundred and eighty pounds. As a result I lay bent in the middle like a sprung bow.

I had started to raise myself onto my elbows when a mule kicked me in the back of the head and I fell back, blinking at the fireflies swarming around my face. For a moment the pain was blinding, but as I lay motionless it ebbed into a sea of blissful warmth that drew me, as it had hours before, toward the brink of unconsciousness. The pounding returned (if indeed it had ever left), but now it seemed muted and distant, like a blacksmith's hammer striking an anvil wrapped in cotton. The effect was mesmeric. This time I didn't fight it. I slept.

The barber was still there when I awoke a second time, or maybe he was back. He was dozing in a paint-spattered wooden chair near the foot of the bed with his legs stretched out in front of him and his hands folded upon the swell of his belly. A kerosene lamp stood on the cracked veneer of the bedside table, hissing and sputtering and casting a liquid glow over the bed and onto the ceiling, where the buzzard still crouched with its injured wing thrust out to the side.

I avoided the temptation to sit up, remembering what had happened the last time. Instead, I unstuck my tongue from the roof of my mouth, rolled it around a little to see if it still worked, and called out Wilson's name. He shifted in his chair, crossed one ankle over the other, and went on sleeping. I tried again.

"Wilson!"

He came awake with a snort, nearly pitching headlong over onto his face when he drew his legs under him and his ankles became tangled with each other. He blinked about, bewildered, and then his eyes fell to me and comprehension dawned in his expression. He grunted like an old dog that had been kicked out of its master's favorite armchair.

"You're alive," he noted morosely. "Thought sure you'd be stone cold by now."

"Sorry to disappoint you."

He smoothed a careful hand over his thinning hair. The band of pink disappeared, then eased back into view as the locks separated again. He eyed me as if he didn't know what to do next. "Suppose you want to eat."

I hadn't thought about it, but as he said it I remembered that as far as I knew I hadn't eaten since breakfast at Arthur's Castle the morning I'd left with my prisoner, and God knew how long ago that had been. I nodded. The movement made me aware of the pounding in my head and I placed a hand against it. It was encircled just below the hairline by a bandage like an Indian headband.

Outside, I heard a wagon rattling past, followed by the grinding sigh of hinges as a large door was swung open or shut nearby. I decided that I was in the back of the barbershop, which was next to the livery stable. No wonder Wilson was so surly, I thought; I was lying in his bed. Carefully I eased myself into a sitting position with my back supported by the brass bedstead. My head weighed fifty pounds.

The barber had left his chair and been swallowed up by the blackness beyond the globe of light thrown by the lamp on the table. Dishes rattled, something wet splattered into something dry, and then he came back bearing a soup plate full of a steaming something which he balanced in one hand while he drew his chair up to the bed and sat down. He lifted out a spoonful of liquid, blew on it, and slid it underneath my nose.

"What is it?" I studied the contents suspiciously. It smelled like boiled rags.

"Venison broth," said the other. "Been cooking all day. Shot it last year and all I got left is jerky. Eat it. Worst it can do is make you heave."

I opened my mouth and he inserted the spoon. It tasted pretty good, but then the judgment of a man half-starved is not to be trusted. I held out my hands for the bowl. He handed it to me and I finished the broth in silence.

"How long was I out?" I handed back the empty vessel and wiped my lips with the graying linen napkin he had given me.

He shrugged and set the bowl and spoon on the table next to the lamp. "Nineteen, twenty hours. When the sheriff brought you in I told him you wouldn't last till sundown. Yours is only the second fractured skull I ever saw. Man who had the first one died two hours after it happened. His didn't look near as bad as yours. What was it, a rock?"

I started to nod, then thought better of it and said, "Yeah."

"How's it feel?"

"Hurts like hell."

"I got something that'll fix that." He got up and walked

back into the gloom, this time in a different direction, probably toward the front where the barbershop was. He had no shirt on over his long-handled underwear and his suspenders flapped loose around his knees. A moment later he returned, this time carrying a tall square bottle in one hand and a shot glass in the other. He sat down and poured a thin stream of pale brownish liquid into the glass. The sickly sweet scent it gave off was overpowering, like that of too many flowers in a room where a corpse lay in state. When the glass was nearly full he thrust it toward me with the same nonchalance with which he had offered me the venison broth. I was suspicious of the human race today. I asked him what it was.

"Laudanum. Take some; it'll ease that ache." He pushed the glass closer. The fumes filled my nostrils and made me drowsy.

I turned my head away. "Pour it back."

"Don't be stubborn." He slid the medicine around toward my lips. "It's the best cure there is."

"I once knew a cowhand who felt that way," I said, looking at him. "He got stomped by a bronc and the doctors fed him that stuff for a solid week to ease the pain, then released him and told him he was good as new. Know what he was doing the last time I saw him? Screaming his lungs out in an insane asylum. The attendants had refused to give him any more of that good medicine. No, thanks. I'd rather have the pain."

"Suit yourself," he said, and drank the stuff himself.

I stared at him, but I don't think he was aware of it. His pupils clouded and his pale lips were turned upward at the corners in a half-smile. It was the expression of a married man who had returned to a favorite mistress. I made a mental note to do my own shaving the next time I came to Staghorn.

Somewhere off in the gloom a doorknob rattled. "Ezra?" The voice belonged to Henry Goodnight, calling from in front of the shop. "Ezra, you asleep? Open up."

That broke the mood. The barber shoved the stopper back into the bottle and shot me a stern look, as if swearing me to secrecy.

"He won't hear it from me," I assured him. "It's not against the law anyway."

That didn't have any effect on him at all. He went out to let Henry in. A bolt squeaked back, there was a muttered conversation, and then the sheriff came striding into the lamp light. He had traded his Prince Albert and fancy vest for a hip-length brown canvas coat with fur at the collar and cuffs and bone buttons that dangled loosely from the threads that held them, and his hat now was a Stetson. He walked as if this was the first time he had used his legs all night. There were dark circles under his eyes and his smile was weary.

"You must have a cast-iron skull," he said. He pulled off a pair of brown leather gloves and stood massaging his right hand with his left. "I had you buried hours ago."

"Where have you been?" I wasn't in the mood for saloon stage banter.

"To the Clark Fork River and back, tracking your prisoner." He swung the paint-spattered chair around and straddled it, folding his arms atop the back. Exhausted or not, he hadn't forgotten to pose. "I don't think you'll have to worry about him any more, because he's as good as dead."

"You shot him?" I started to get up, then remembered the mule waiting to kick my brains out and settled back.

"Why waste a bullet? I followed his trail north as far as Glacier Pass, where it swung west and headed straight into the mountains. I figure he's on his way to Canada by a

route where he won't meet too many people. He'll meet a
lot more than he reckoned on once the Flatheads find out
there's a white man in their midst. He won't live to see
Canada."

I felt a chill, but not from the thought of Brainard's re-
ception at the hands of the Indians. A vapor of cold air had
begun to waft from Henry's clothes over to me. The tem-
perature outside must have dropped considerably since I'd
returned to Staghorn, as there was a light dusting of snow
on the sheriff's hat and coat, now turning to beads of moisture in the heat of the shop's invisible stove. I shivered
slightly beneath the thin stuff of my nightshirt. I decided
that Henry had helped Wilson undress me and put me to
bed; the thought of the little barber attempting it alone
was just too ludicrous.

"Is the situation that bad?" I asked Henry.

"Take a good look around you," he said. "There isn't a
homesteader in the area who'd step outside his house without a rifle or a gun on his hip. It started after Doc Bernstein got killed, and since last spring when all those braves
were scalped in that hunting party, it's been just a matter
of when Two Sisters thinks the time is right to strike.
That's what I tried to tell that bounty hunter Church, but
he wouldn't listen. Likely his scalp is already decorating a
pole in some brave's lodge."

There was a moment of silence while he appeared to be
searching for something else to say. Absent-mindedly he resumed massaging his right hand with his left where they
rested on the back of the chair. He saw me watching,
looked down at his hands, saw what he was doing, and
dropped them to his knees.

"What's the matter with your hand?" I asked him.

"Nothing. I think I sprained my wrist when I pistol-
whipped Ira Longbow." He got up. "Anyway, you can stop

worrying about Leslie Brainard. He won't be strangling any more wives."

"Tell that to Judge Blackthorne."

His laugh was theatrical, as was everything else about him, but it was genuine and it did me good to hear it. "You'll think of a good excuse," he said. "You always do. Meanwhile, leave your head on that pillow and don't let Ezra get too close to you with a razor in his hand. He really wants that bed." He strode out past the barber. A moment later I heard the front door clap shut.

Wilson came over and returned the chair to its original position at the foot of the bed. "You need anything else?" He seemed gratified when I told him I didn't. "Chamber pot's under the bed," he said. "Holler if you need help." He settled himself into the chair, squirmed around until he found the hollow he wanted, and was asleep again within five minutes.

I waited until I was sure he wouldn't wake up, then, slowly—not so much because of him as because of my head, which had settled into an almost bearable throb—I peeled aside the threadbare counterpane that had been covering me and swung my feet to the floor. The boards felt like ice. For a moment I sat there, preparing myself. Then I took a deep breath and stood up.

A shotgun exploded deep inside my head, spraying the walls of my skull with red-hot pellets that burst in turn behind my eyes and dizzied me so that I had to clutch at the bedstead to keep from falling. My stomach did a slow turn, like a whale rolling over in deep water. Then, with excruciating slowness, the pain began to subside. At length my vision returned and I found myself standing with knees bent, holding onto the bedpost with a kitten's grip. I welcomed the throbbing inside my head as an old friend.

After a few minutes of searching, I found my clothes in

a heap at the bottom of a scarred wardrobe in which there was nothing else but Ezra Wilson's shirt drooping from a wire hanger on the rod. I dressed, easing the hat on last so that it topped the bandage, and went out through the darkened barbershop. Wilson hadn't stirred.

The snow was an inch deep on the street and still falling. The cold air felt good on my aching head. I spent ten minutes banging on the door of the mercantile before Bart Goddard came storming out from the back, wearing his nightshirt and carrying a double-barreled shotgun, and another twenty getting him to open up and sell me enough supplies for a two-week journey. As I was leaving with the bundles he muttered something that I wouldn't have stood for had I been in any condition to do something about it. I pretended I hadn't heard him and headed back down the street toward the livery stable, where I was in luck. There was a light on in the office and the old man was awake.

My cash supply was running low by this time. I'd brought along a little extra for emergencies, but as I hadn't anticipated any the extra wasn't much. So instead of renting a better horse I paid the old man for the care he'd given the chestnut mare, brought in by the sheriff, and asked him to saddle it and load up the supplies I had brought with me while I called on Henry. I felt strange going through all these familiar motions; but for the hour and the way my head felt, it might have been the day before yesterday.

The door to the sheriff's office was locked, but there was a light on inside. I knocked.

"Just a minute," called Henry's voice.

It seemed longer before the door was opened. He was hatless and in his shirtsleeves, and he had either just put his gun belt back on or had been in the process of removing it when I'd knocked; the thong with which he usually tied down his holster was hanging loose down the seam of his pants leg. He was surprised to see me.

"No lectures, Henry," I said, when his expression became disapproving. I went past him into the office.

His desk was bare except for a pan of hot water standing on top of it. Next to it was a folded towel—a thick one, most likely stolen from Arthur's Castle. I dipped a couple of fingers into the steaming water and put them to my mouth. They tasted of salt.

"How's the wrist feel now that you've soaked it?" I asked the sheriff.

"Better." He closed the door. "What are you doing out of bed?"

"I came to borrow a revolver and a rifle. Got any to spare?"

"You're not going after Brainard."

"No," I said acidly, "I just thought I'd do a little rabbit hunting up in the mountains. It'll be good for my head. Of course I'm going after him. That's what Blackthorne pays me for."

"He's dead, Page. You'd just be wasting your time."

"If he's dead I've got to see his body. The judge won't settle for anything less and neither will I. Do I get the guns or not?"

He got his key ring out of the desk, went over to the gun rack, and unlocked a padlock securing the chain that held his half-dozen rifles and one shotgun in place. "Which do you want?" he growled.

"I'll take the Henry, if that's the best you've got."

He tossed me the carbine, a slightly battered piece with a triangular chunk missing from the stock. From a drawer in the bottom of the rack he took a box of shells. I accepted it and loaded the rifle. "What about a revolver and gun belt?" I reminded him.

"This is the only other one I have," he said, handing me a gun and holster he'd taken from the drawer. "This means I can't get mine fixed until you come back. If you come back."

I slid the revolver from its holster. It was a Peacemaker like his other one, but unlike his other one the butt was plain wood without a trace of ivory. I freed the cylinder and thumbed it around. It was loaded. I strapped on the belt. "Care to come with me?"

He laughed shortly. "I'm not paid to commit suicide," he said. "Besides, that's out of my jurisdiction."

"That never stopped you before."

"No, thanks."

I nodded, eyeing him thoughtfully. Suddenly I whipped the Colt out of its holster and pointed it at him.

His reflexes were sharp. No sooner had I made the move than his right hand swung down and scooped up his own gun. Then it spun from his grip and clattered loudly to the floor.

For a long moment we stood staring at each other, me over the barrel of the gun he had given me, Henry with his right arm crooked and not a weapon within reach. The ticking of the clock on the wall behind his head sounded like pistol reports in the silence.

I holstered the Colt. "Rheumatism, right?"

"It comes and goes." He sank to his heels and retrieved his gun. His right hand reminded me of a gardener's claw, it was that bent. "How'd you guess?" he asked, when he was standing again and the gun was in its holster.

"You were too quick to say no when I asked you to come with me," I explained. "You like action too much to give me that answer that soon. And when I asked you about your wrist, you changed the subject. How long have you had it?"

"A year and a half, maybe longer. Lately it's been getting worse. If it wasn't for my reputation, I suppose I'd have been dead long ago."

"You can't get by on your reputation forever."

"I know it." There was annoyance in his tone. "What else can I do? I'm too old to punch cattle. The only other thing I know how to do is use a gun, and now I'm losing even that. Where do I go, to the Old Sheriffs' Home? There aren't enough old sheriffs around to make a thing like that worthwhile. We don't live that long."

"Who else knows?"

"No one. Doc Bernstein knew—he guessed it, just like you—but there was nothing he could do for it, except prescribe laudanum when the pain got too bad. I tried it once, and it put me out for twelve hours. I haven't had any since. I'll take my chances with the rheumatism."

I let it drop. "Watch your back, Henry," I said. "Tell Wilson I'll be back to pay him." I slung the Henry under my arm and headed for the door.

"That's what you think," he retorted.

Tracing was impossible after the snowfall, but if what Henry had told me was true, there was only one way Brainard could have gone. West of the Clark Fork, a couple of hundred thousand years before even the Indians came, glaciers had carved a wedge five hundred feet wide through the Bitterroot Mountains. From the point where the ice had emerged, the pass took a ragged turn north toward Canada, narrowing as it progressed until there was barely enough room for a man on horseback to squeeze between the encroaching pillars of rock. In another million years it would close up tight. For now, however, it was the shortest available route through the range in the direction Brainard was heading, and it was more than a safe bet that he would choose to take it rather than attempt to push my buckskin over the nearly vertical mountains. I reached the opening shortly before noon and dismounted to take a look around. That's when I found the fresh tracks.

There were a lot of them near the northern edge of the opening, churning the snow into dull piles and exposing the brown earth beneath. They represented six or seven horses, none of them shod. A hunting party, I judged, returning with its game from a trip into the plains. Flatheads, or they would have avoided the mountains entirely. The tracks were only a few hours old. While studying them, I felt a crawling sensation between my shoulder blades and wondered if I was being watched. I stood up and scanned the peaks, but they were the same color as the sky, and the outline of a human head would have been impossible to see against the woodash gray of the clouds. I decided that if someone was watching it was too late to do anything about it. I mounted up and steered the chestnut into the pass, taking what advantage I could of the narrow strip of shadow left by the pale glimmer of the sun directly above my head.

It was late afternoon when I found them. The horse smelled them first and shied, tossing its head and chortling through its nostrils. Then I caught a whiff. A musty smell, like you get when you split a deer carcass down the middle and spread its ribs. My stomach, empty now of the venison broth I'd had that morning, began to work. I breathed through my mouth and coaxed the mare forward into a stand of low pines up ahead.

Leslie Brainard, what was left of him, hung naked by his wrists from a buckhide thong wound around the trunk of a pine six feet above the ground. His legs had been pulled back so that he straddled the trunk, his ankles lashed tight behind it. Ragged stripes of purple glistened from his collarbone to his pelvis where the flesh had been torn in strips from his body. His eyes started from their sockets farther than I had thought they could without actually popping out onto his cheeks. His mouth was wide open as if he had been screaming, but his screams had been incoherent because his tongue had been cut out. A hole the size of a fifty-dollar gold piece showed black and empty between his breasts. He would have welcomed it.

His tormentors hadn't outlived him by more than a few minutes. Five of the seven Indians lay where they had fallen; the other two had managed to crawl several yards through the snow before expiring. Behind them, the trails they had left were streaked with red. None of the corpses had been stripped of furs or buckskins, which would have been the case had the attackers been their own kind. Four still had weapons in their hands. All they were missing was their scalps.

I swung out of my saddle, holding onto the reins to keep the mare from galloping away in its panic. The snow was trampled with footprints. One, a blurred oval such as a fur boot might leave, was nearly large enough for me to stand in with both feet. At first I thought it was a normal print that had grown with the melting of the snow around it, but then I found more of them and I remembered.

I tethered the horse to a juniper bush, pulled off a glove, and squatted to feel for a pulse at the throat of the Indian lying nearest me. The snow was no colder than his flesh. In his abdomen he sported a hole identical to the one in Brainard's chest. I inspected the others. Same story, although the holes weren't always in the same place. One of the Indians, a crawler, had a second wound in the back of his head, puckered with powder burns, as if his killer had walked right up to him and placed the muzzle against his skull before pulling the trigger. This time Mountain That Walks had left no one to tell the tale.

My first intimation that I wasn't alone with the corpses came when I heard a squeaking footfall in the snow behind me. I swung around, drawing my gun.

"A mistake, white skin." The words were grunted rather than spoken, as though torn from a throat that had not used the language in years.

The way out of the pines was sealed off by a semicircle of mottled horses, astride the bare backs of which sat a dozen fur-clad riders whose features looked oddly alike within the frames of their shaggy headpieces. Their hair was long and black and arranged in braids hanging down onto their chests, their eyes black slits in the glare of the minimal sunlight coming off the fresh snow. They were the corpses on the ground around me come to life. The only difference was that each of them was armed with a carbine, and that every one was trained on me. Almost every one.

The one that wasn't was slung over the shoulder of the Indian in the center, the one who had spoken. This one had a moon face, fleshy for a brave, in which not a crease or a wrinkle showed, making it look like a child's India rubber balloon with features painted on it. The impression of lifelessness was carried further by the fact that the face wore no expression at all. His mouth was bland, his eyes like doll's eyes and without brows. They watched me unblinkingly. For all its emptiness, though, the face carried more of a threat than the scowling visages of his companions with weathered rifle stocks pressed against their cheeks and index fingers poised around the triggers.

I returned the Colt to its holster. I needed no more convincing to know that I'd wandered into a trap set by Rocking Wolf, nephew of Two Sisters and next chief of the Flathead nation.

CHAPTER FIVE

For two beats after I put away the gun, no one moved. We might have been snow sculptures in that lonely glade. Then, at a signal from Rocking Wolf, the brave mounted at his right lowered his gun and trotted over to me, where he sat looking down at me with an expectant scowl.

"You will surrender your weapons," directed the Indian in command. His English was ponderous but correct.

Thinking that it was becoming increasingly difficult for me to hold onto a firearm, I unbuckled my gun belt and handed it up to the brave. There was another long silence while his eyes searched me from head to foot. At length they settled upon the hilt of the knife protruding above the top of my right boot. The scowl became ominous. I stooped, drew the knife from its sheath, and gave it to him, handle first.

While the brave had been engaged in disarming me, Rocking Wolf had nodded again, this time to a savage at his left, who swung past my skitterish mount and hooked the Henry out of its scabbard, then tossed it to his superior. Rocking Wolf caught it in one hand and examined it perfunctorily. With a shrug he handed it to another brave.

"I do not applaud your preference in firearms," he told me. "What is your name, and what have you to do with the thing that has happened here this day?"

I told him my name. "As for the rest," I added, "I prefer to talk it over with Two Sisters. Where is your chief?"

Rocking Wolf barked something in Salish. Immediately the brave who had relieved me of my revolver and knife reached down and snatched a handful of my collar, thrusting the point of the latter weapon against my jugular as he did so. His hands smelled of rancid bear grease.

"Perhaps opening your throat will show us the way to your tongue," said the chief's nephew.

The bite of the knife acted as a spur to my already racing thoughts. "Killing me will gain you nothing, Rocking Wolf," I said hoarsely. "Whereas allowing me to live may lead you to the hiding place of Mountain That Walks."

The forbidden name brought a reaction from all who understood the language, even Rocking Wolf. Again there was a long silence. I felt a drop of blood trickle down my throat and into my collar.

"How is it that you know my name, white skin?"

I hesitated, allowing my eyes to slide toward the Indian holding the knife. At a nod from his superior the brave withdrew the blade and relinquished his grip on my collar.

"I used to run into you and your brother, Yellow Horn, in the mountains when you were hunting." I rubbed my throat, smearing the blood. "That was many years ago. Few words passed between us at those times."

"I do not remember you."

"It's likely you didn't notice me. I was always with Bear Anderson, him who you call Mountain That Walks."

For an instant, Rocking Wolf let slip his mask, revealing the naked hatred that writhed beneath. Nine rifles were poised to fire; there was a beat during which I was one harsh syllable away from death. Then he retreated behind the India rubber façade once again.

"You are either very brave or very foolish to tell me that," he said. "I have not yet decided which is the case."

"Do we have a bargain?"

"What makes you think I value your knowledge? The murderer of my people has left a clear trail to follow, and we are expert trackers."

"Now who's being foolish? Nightfall is less than two hours away. Even Salish can't track a man in the dark. By tomorrow the snow will have returned to cover the trail. I grew up with Anderson, remember; I know how he thinks. I alone can lead you to his lair."

He studied me in silence. His thoughts were impossible to read. After an eternity he looked to the brave with the knife and gave him a curt order. Reluctantly, the brave backed his horse away from me.

"Mount your horse," Rocking Wolf directed. "You will get your meeting with the chief."

I waited until all weapons were put away, then stepped forward to untie the chestnut.

It was the work of five minutes for the braves to gather up their dead and sling them over the backs of their horses. When that was done, Leslie Brainard was left alone to decorate the tree where he had met his merciful end. By morning the wolves and coyotes would finish the job that had been started by the Indians.

"Where is Yellow Horn?" I asked Rocking Wolf, once I was in the saddle. "I don't see him in your party."

"My brother is dead," he said. "Killed last winter by Mountain That Walks." He gave his horse a kick and led the way north.

The pass inclined steadily upward to about six thousand feet, where it leveled out, yielding what would have been a spectacular view of the sunset over the Bitterroot had it not been for the thickening veil of clouds that reduced the violent reds and purples to a vague rust on the horizon. Soon even that was gone, and from then on we felt our way forward with only the aid of the snow's own mysterious source of illumination. An hour after sundown it began to snow again, this time in large wet flakes that slithered down our faces and made sizzling noises when they struck the ground. I dug my chin into my chest for warmth. Around me, the Indians rode straight as andirons; in their bearskins they remained as warm as if they hadn't left their fire-lit lodges.

The Flathead camp was laid out across a broad spot in the pass, between two cliffs of sheer rock. Only the tops of the temporary animal-hide structures were visible above the snow. Here and there a torch burned, its flame flaring and faltering beneath the snow's untiring assault. A hundred yards before we reached the camp we were stopped by a rifle-toting sentry atop the east cliff, who addressed our leader in rapid Salish.

Rocking Wolf answered him in the same tongue, gesticulating in my direction and snarling a string of words that didn't sound much like compliments. The sentry lowered his weapon and waved us on.

"You're late getting out of the mountains this year," I remarked as we entered camp.

"That is because Two Sisters cannot be moved." Rocking Wolf kept his eyes trained straight ahead of him. "Ten suns ago he was thrown by his horse. His injuries have yet to heal."

A scruffy dog of uncertain ancestry came bouncing out from behind one of the lodges and announced our arrival in raucous barks. It was joined by another, and soon we were surrounded by mongrels of every size and description, snapping at our heels and raising enough racket to bestir the corpses on the backs of the party's mounts. Here and there a flap was pulled aside and a half-naked brave stepped out of his lodge to stare at us with suspicious eyes.

The chief's lodge, a squat cone made of buffalo hide and

bearskin sewn together and stretched over six stout poles
bound together at the top by a strip of uncured leather,
was no grander than those that surrounded it. A colorless
haze of heat drifted out through the opening in the top,
causing the crossed ends of the poles to shimmer like
sunken pilings at the bottom of a shallow pond. Rocking
Wolf dismounted before the lodge and, out of habit,
landed a glancing blow with the sole of his right moccasin
boot alongside the head of a black-muzzled mutt that had
gotten too close. The dog shrieked and drew its upper lip
back over its yellowed fangs, but it shrank away. The Indian exchanged a few low words with the fur-clad brave
guarding the entrance, who ducked inside for a moment,
then returned and nodded curtly. Rocking Wolf told me
to stay where I was and entered the lodge through the low
flap.

News that a white man had been brought in alive along
with the corpses of the missing hunting party had spread
quickly throughout the camp. Everywhere I looked I met a
hostile face, leaving me with little doubt about who they
believed was responsible. I thought of Leslie Brainard's
fate and wondered if they could have anything worse in
store for me.

The wails of the women were conspicuous by their absence; I came to realize after a moment that there were
few, if any, squaws in camp. Probably they were waiting
for their men back at the permanent village west of the
Bitterroot. That was proof enough that the prospect of
crossing the mountains was no longer a casual one now
that they were part of Bear Anderson's domain. The
thought didn't gratify me. A savage afraid, like an animal
cornered, was a thing best left alone.

The quickening snow had put out the last of the torches
by the time the chief's nephew emerged from the lodge

and signaled for me to enter. I dismounted amid a chorus of threatening growls and elbowed my way through the throng, expecting any time to feel the burning pain of a knife blade being shoved between my ribs.

But the aura of command that surrounded the chief's lodge was too great, and presently I found myself blinking in the light of the fire that burned in the center of the cone. After the dimness of the snow-covered landscape outside, it was some moments before my eyes could discern anything in the gloom that surrounded that crackling brightness. Meanwhile, I occupied myself by listening to the voice that addressed me as soon as I entered.

"You're far from home, Page Murdock." It was a dry voice; something that had been left too close to the fire so that all the moisture had been allowed to bake away, leaving only the brittle shell. It handled English with less difficulty than Rocking Wolf, which was no surprise. During his fifty-odd years, Chief Two Sisters had learned to speak three languages fluently.

"Farther than you think, Chief," I said after a moment. I fished my badge out of my breast pocket and held it up in the firelight. "I'm a deputy U.S. marshal operating out of Helena. The man your braves were torturing when they were surprised by Mountain That Walks was my prisoner. He's the reason I'm here."

The fire hissed and belched while Two Sisters digested the information I'd given him. Gradually, I was able to make out the lines and finally the details of a lean figure sitting up on a straw pallet on the other side of the flames, his back supported against one of the sturdy poles and a buffalo robe drawn up to his chest. His eyes were black hollows beneath a high, square brow. The shifting firelight threw his equally square chin and sharp cheekbones into relief against the corrugated parchment of the rest of his face. He had a wide, firm mouth and a nose with a crushed bridge, as if at some time in the distant past it had come up hard against the flat of an enemy tomahawk. His hair was shoulder-length but unbraided, the color of tarnished silver. The term Flathead being a misnomer foisted upon the Montana Salish by the early pioneers, there were no signs of the artificial flattening of the skull practiced by some western tribes. His breathing, loud in the seclusion of the lodge, was even but careful, as I suppose any man's would be after he had broken several ribs falling from his horse.

There was a third party in the lodge, a squat, broad-shouldered brave whose features were impossible to make out as he stood almost completely enveloped in shadow beside his seated chief. His chest was naked and powerful, leathery slabs of muscle glistening beneath the obligatory coating of bear grease. When he moved his head I caught a glimpse of firelight glinting off the buffalo horns of his headdress. That would make him the medicine man. Knowing that, I didn't have to see his face to guess what he thought of my presence in camp. There isn't a medicine man west of Buffalo Bill's show who doesn't view all white men as a threat to his authority.

"This man you say you were hunting," spoke up Two Sisters. "Which of your laws did he break?"

I told him. His scowl carved deep lines from his nostrils to the corners of his mouth.

"A foolish crime. We Salish beat our squaws when they make us angry, but we do not kill them. What's to be gained?" He sighed, easing his breath out between his cracked ribs. "It's a shame that Mountain That Walks arrived when he did to put an end to his suffering. The fate the hunting party had planned for him was far more fitting. He is the one responsible for your injury?"

I put a hand to my head, touching the bandage beneath the brim of my hat. The pounding had become so much a part of me that I'd forgotten I was wearing it. I nodded.

"He had no firearms?"

"He did after he hit me. I saw no sign of them where he was killed. At the time I assumed Bear Anderson had taken them, but they could just as easily have been picked up by Rocking Wolf and his party."

Two Sisters shook his head. "My brother's son says the only weapons he saw were those that had been carried by the dead braves. Their horses were also missing, perhaps frightened off by the shots." He paused. A stick of wood near the heart of the fire separated with a loud report, sending up a geyser of sparks and bathing the chief's face in brief, fiery brilliance. His eyes were sad. "It's a bad thing to have happen," he said. "Tomorrow I will have no choice but to call a council of war."

"Not if I can lead you to the lair of Mountain That Walks."

The flare had died, returning his face to shadowy patchwork. "Rocking Wolf has told me of your boast," he said. "How will you do this?"

"How do you hunt any game? By knowing its habits. I spent a third of my life hunting those mountains with Anderson. His movements are predictable. Depending on the weather and the shifting of the game he lives on, I can place him within a few miles at any given time."

"Remarkable. And where is he now?"

I smiled. "You don't really expect an answer to that."

"I suppose not." He returned the smile, faintly. "I'm curious to know why you are offering your service in this matter."

"I'm always willing to help when the price is right. In this case it's my life."

He thought that over. Outside, the snow settled onto the

sides of the lodge with a sound like frying bacon. At last he spoke.

"You're probably lying, but I can't afford to pass up any opportunity to avoid war with the whites at a time when we are so poorly prepared. It has been five of your years since the bulk of my people was moved forcibly to the valley you call the Flathead, two days' ride east of this camp. Our numbers now are small." He swept a hand across his face, as if to erase the memory. It was a neat piece of acting. "You and Rocking Wolf will leave at dawn tomorrow. You have until the next moon to return either with news of where to find Mountain That Walks or with his body slung across a saddle."

"Just Rocking Wolf? You must trust me."

"A party would attract too much attention. As for Rocking Wolf, he is the best of my warriors. I would advise you not to attempt an escape."

"You didn't worry about attracting attention last year, when you headed up the bunch that killed Doc Bernstein outside Staghorn," I reminded him.

"The old white man," he said, after a pause. "I remember the incident. He gave us no choice. We had reason to believe that he was harboring Mountain That Walks after one of our party had wounded him. We asked for permission to search his dwelling. He was going to shoot."

"What about his wife and child? Where they going to shoot?"

He studied me for a moment without speaking. The chief used silence like a weapon. "You're an emotional man, Page Murdock. I didn't realize that before."

"And was Mountain That Walks there?"

"No. Apparently we were mistaken."

I didn't carry it any further. The confrontation had

given me a clear idea of the boundaries of his patience, and they weren't as broad as they'd seemed. Nothing about him was as it seemed. I changed the subject.

"I need food and a place to sleep. Can you fix me up?"

"My nephew will see to your needs," he said. "One more question."

I had turned to duck through the flap. I stopped and looked back at him.

"Since you know so much, perhaps you can tell me why a party of four white men was seen two days southwest of here by my scouts the day before yesterday. Is this a new trick on the part of your army to rob my people of their birthright?"

He spoke casually, but I could tell that he had been waiting to ask the question ever since I'd appeared in the lodge. I pretended to give it some thought, though of course I already knew the answer. "Was one of them a small man wearing a big hat and a long yellow coat?"

"The scouts described a small man with a big hat. There was no mention of a coat, yellow or any other color."

"He probably traded it for something warmer. His name is Church, and he has a warrant signed by the President for the arrest of Mountain That Walks. Two of the men with him are his partners. As for all of them being white, your scouts need glasses; the fourth is a half-breed who calls himself Ira Longbow." I hesitated, letting the silence work against the chief for a change. "He claims to be your son."

If I expected any kind of reaction to that last piece of information, I was disappointed. Two Sisters could have given Rocking Wolf poker lessons when he wanted to. Finally he nodded. That could have meant that he believed me, but it could just as well have been a sign of satisfaction at hearing an expected lie. In any case, he didn't return to the subject.

"The next moon," he reminded me. "I can wait no longer. By then the first blizzard will be on its way to block the passes with snow and ice. We must leave the mountains by then or be trapped. When we return in the spring, we will be carrying arms and wearing paint for war with the whites. Much to my regret."

I left, my back tingling beneath the medicine man's hostile scrutiny.

A sour-featured brave escorted me like the prisoner I was to a lodge near the camp's center. There I was handed an earthen dish heaped with chunks of lean, bloody meat by an old squaw whose cracked pumpkin of a face told me she had borne worse dangers than those offered by Bear Anderson's mountains. I ate hungrily, not pausing to wonder which of the dogs that had greeted me earlier was going into my stomach; to a man in my condition it tasted like tenderest sirloin. When it was finished and the dish was taken away, I stretched out fully clothed on a flat straw pallet beside the fire and drew a mildewed blanket up to my chin.

I was prepared to spend the night staring up at the cloud-lathered sky through the opening in the top of the lodge. As it turned out, however, I had little trouble getting to sleep. So great was my exhaustion that nothing could have kept me awake, not even the fact that I didn't have the slightest idea of where to find Bear Anderson or his lair.

CHAPTER SIX

"You are leading me in circles, white skin." Rocking Wolf spoke flatly and seemingly without emotion, but the emotion was there, in his words. They dripped cold fury.

The sun had risen dazzlingly over twelve inches of fresh snow, shining through the spots where the wind had slashed the cloud cover into fibrous shreds and turning the uninterrupted vista of white into a blazing brilliance that hurt the eyes and did little toward relieving my headache. We had followed the paso northward until the flanking cliffs fell away, at which point we had taken a turn to the west and swung lazily in the direction from which we had come. It was midmorning before we stopped at the top of a gentle rise and looked out over the Christmas-painting scenery of crystallized trees and blue-shadowed drifts. I was still stuck with the broken-down chestnut mare, while Rocking Wolf had secured himself a fresh mount that morning from his stable of painted stallions—a situation meant to discourage any plans I might have entertained about escaping. Over his shoulder was slung a Winchester with a shattered and thong-bound stock. In the distance a river etched its way southward through the foothills, its chocolate color startling against the carved whiteness of its banks. To the south, clouds drifting across the mountaintops tore themselves lengthwise along the razor edges of the peaks. The air was brittle.

"No circles," I corrected him. My breath hung in vapor.

"We're just taking the easy way south. By now the narrow part of the pass is piled up with drifts three feet high. If you'd rather flounder your way through that, you're welcome to try, but I'll be waiting for you at the other end."

"How do I know you are not leading me into a trap? You have already admitted that Mountain That Walks is your friend."

"Was my friend. I haven't seen him in over fifteen years."

He looked at me, and I got the impression that he was smirking behind the coarse scarf that swathed the lower part of his face, leaving only his eyes visible between it and his bearskin headpiece. "And does the white man find it necessary to see his friends every day to ensure that they remain friends?" he asked.

"Look around," I said. "If I were going to lead you into a trap, would I have chosen this area? From here you can see ten miles in every direction. The pass would have been a far better place for an ambush."

"Where are we going?"

I nodded toward the mountains to the south. "Straight up. If I know Bear, he'll be heading where no Indian in his right mind would follow him. This time of year a mountain goat would have trouble getting around on the high rocks."

"That is a long way to go if we are to return by the next moon."

"You can talk to your uncle about that," I said. "He's the one who set the time limit." I urged the mare forward down the slope.

The wind began to rise about noon, and for the rest of the day it blew in ever-increasing gusts, bringing snow swirling down from the sides of the mountains and rippling the wet stuff in the flat spots until they resembled sheets of corrugated iron. After a while my face grew numb and I fell into the habit of pinching it from time to time between gloved fingers to make sure the skin wasn't frostbitten. Steam rose from the mare's neck and withers.

Night fell without warning, the way it does in the mountains; one minute we were riding along through snow tinted orange by the wallowing sun, our shadows stretching out a mile to our left, and the next we were plunged into darkness. We made camp on a slope, using a stand of jack pine for a windbreak and building a tiny fire with the aid of boughs from a dead tree, over which we warmed our stiff fingers. Rocking Wolf watched from a safe distance while I used a knife borrowed from him to pare off a couple of slices of bacon from the small slab I had bought in Staghorn. I cut out more than was needed and slipped the extra slices inside my coat to keep them from freezing. When I was finished he held out his hand for the weapon. I returned it reluctantly. My skillet having disappeared along with my horse the day Brainard got away, I strung the slices on a stick and roasted them over the flame. This done, I offered one to the Indian. He shook his head, holding up a three-inch length of jerky which he had taken from inside his bearskin where he had been keeping it warm beneath his arm.

"Suit yourself," I said, crunching the crisp bacon between my teeth. "There won't be many more hot meals where we're going. We can't take the chance of having Bear smell wood smoke once we hit the mountains."

"White men." Rocking Wolf ground away contemptuously at the tough jerky. "How do you expect to conquer the Indian when you insist upon taking all the conveniences of home with you wherever you go? Give a Salish a knife and a piece of jerky, send him out into the wilderness, and he will come back two moons later as healthy as he was when he left."

I let that one slide while I studied the strip of bacon remaining on the stick. "What do you plan to do with Mountain That Walks once you've got him?"

He paused in mid-chew. His browless eyes glittered in the light of the little fire: "That decision belongs to the chief," he said. "When I was a boy, not yet strong enough to draw a bow, I saw the punishment of a white soldier who had been captured in the act of raping a squaw. He was a big man, like you, with big hard hands and a face like cracked leather. I think he was what you would call a sergeant. The braves stripped him and turned him over to the women, who have their own way of dealing with the crime of which he was guilty.

"It is a compliment to his strength and training that he was still alive when it was over. He begged to be killed. The braves did not oblige. They left him lying there until he ceased to beg." He went on chewing. "This was for the crime of rape. I imagine Two Sisters has something much more fitting in mind for the murderer of our people."

"Do your people enjoy seeing suffering that much?"

"We enjoy it no more than the whites. When a man commits a crime among your people, he is usually compelled to hang from a rope by his neck until he chokes his last. Our punishments are neither worse nor better. They are just different." He finished eating and rolled himself up in the buffalo robe he used for a blanket. "Sleep," he said. "We will move again at dawn."

I sat there a moment longer, gazing at the uneaten slice of bacon. In the firelight it took on a reddish glow, as though it were dripping with fresh blood. I thrust it inside my coat and made ready for bed.

Staying awake was harder than I'd anticipated. In many ways, riding a horse all day long is more exhausting than walking for the same length of time, and in spite of the cold and the hardness of the ground I had all I could do to keep my eyelids from falling shut of their own weight. I stuck it out for the better part of an hour, and then I got quietly to my feet and picked up my saddle, holding onto the cinch lest the buckle jingle. Rocking Wolf lay motionless beneath his buffalo robe on the other side of the guttering fire. With the saddle under my arm and the blanket and saddlebags slung over my shoulder I stepped cautiously through the wet snow to where our horses were standing in the shelter of the pines, mine tethered, the Indian's hobbled. I gazed longingly at the painted stallion for a moment, but I was no bareback rider, and saddling it was out of the question as it was unfamiliar with the procedure and would undoubtedly have balked and alerted its master. Besides, I was getting used to the chestnut, which says something for the adaptability of human nature. I saddled the mare.

I had my foot in the stirrup and was about to swing my right leg over when something piled into me from behind and carried me with it to the ground, emptying my lungs upon impact and clapping my jaws shut with a jarring snap. The mare whinnied and tried to rear, pulling taut the reins that held it. Snow sifted down from the pine's shivering boughs. My skull rang. Dazed, I lay on my face in the snow for a long moment, grinding pieces of what had been a perfectly good molar between my teeth. Then I scrambled to my feet and swung around, fists clenched. I stopped when Rocking Wolf placed the muzzle of the Colt I had borrowed from Henry Goodnight against my forehead and drew the hammer back with a sound like a walnut being crushed.

"I wondered what had happened to that," I said finally. I let my hands drop to my sides.

Moonlight drenched the Indian in silver, but it might just as well have been dark for all the expression he wore. His bearskin and leggings were covered with snow from his tackle. "You might have died, white skin," he said. "I would not like to see that happen. Not until we have found Mountain That Walks."

He held the gun on me while I unsaddled the chestnut, and kept me covered all the way back to camp. Then he put the weapon away inside his bearskin and settled down on his side of the glowing ashes as if nothing had happened to disturb him. His seeming carelessness didn't tempt me. It would have pleased him to shoot me in the leg during an escape attempt; I would still be alive to lead him to his quarry and would give him less trouble. Wrapped in my blanket, I lay back and stared at the sky. The moon, shot with clouds like black arteries in a blind man's eye, was full. Tomorrow it would begin to wane, eventually to be replaced by a new moon.

"Don't remind me," I muttered, and drew the blanket over my head. But that was too much like what they do to corpses, so I pulled it down and turned over onto my left side.

When day broke, crisp and cold as the leftover slice of bacon I had for breakfast, we had left the camp far behind and were starting up the grade that wound into the mountains. The wind had died down, but that was only temporary, the lull before the big blow. The air stung my nostrils and the sun was so bright coming off the clean surface of the snow that I was forced to ride with my eyes squeezed shut most of the time to keep from going snowblind. It was because of this that I failed to see the tracks on the northern slope until my horse was right on top of them.

I turned to the Indian, but he had already noticed them. He nodded once, curtly. I obeyed his unspoken command and dismounted for a closer look.

Four horses had trampled the snow into a trail of slush that girded the mountain from east to west.

"Have you ever known Mountain That Walks to travel with companions?" I asked Rocking Wolf.

"Never." He bounded to the ground and squatted for a moment beside the trail. "Nor have I known him to ride a shod horse. You have laid a poor trap, white skin." He drew out the revolver and pointed it at me.

"Put it away," I said, wearily. "I thought you Indians were supposed to have such good eyesight. Can't you see that one of these men is wounded?" I pointed out the spots of blood that peppered the snow.

He spent a long time studying the crimson specks. Finally he returned the gun to the inside of his bearskin and stood up. "We will follow them," he said. "If it is a trick, you are the one who will pay."

We didn't have far to go. Two miles later the Indian reined in and signaled for me to do the same. He sniffed the air. I followed his lead.

"Wood smoke," I said.

He didn't reply, but kicked his horse gently and together we rode forward at a walk around the bend of the mountain. We halted at the top of a rise that fell away before us into a fan-shaped hollow, at the bottom of which three men sat huddled around a fire at the base of a lone pine. A fourth lay wrapped in blankets nearby. Their horses, tethered to the tree, craned their necks to nibble at the needles on the lower branches above their heads.

"White men do not belong in the wilderness," observed Rocking Wolf in a low murmur. "It is a foolish camper who kindles his fire beneath a tree heavy with snow."

"Not if he doesn't want anyone to know he's there," I said. "Those branches do a pretty good job of breaking up the smoke so that it can't be seen from a distance."

"You know them?"

I nodded. "It's Church and his bunch, the Strakeys and Ira Longbow. That's Church, the small one with his back to us. They're the party Two Sisters' scouts reported seeing a few days back."

"Will they give us trouble?"

"They want what we want. Of course they'll give us trouble."

We were picking our way down the slope when one of the tethered horses spotted us and began snorting. Church, who had been facing away from the rise, sprang up and spun on his heel, drawing his gun as he did so. On the other side of the fire, Ira Longbow rose slowly with his Dance in his hand. He wore the black Spanish hat I'd seen earlier, low over his eyes in the manner of a caballero, but it didn't help; he still looked like a half-breed. The third man, Homer Strakey, Sr., watched us from a kneeling position beside his son's prostrate form. As before, I was unable to tell if he was wearing any weapon at all. Which made him the one to watch.

We stopped five yards from camp, and for a space the horses' fidgeting was the only sound for miles. Then Strakey, Jr., began moaning in a low voice and broke the tension.

"Page Murdock." A grin flickered across Church's face, but it was just his peculiar tick manifesting itself once again. He made no move to holster the gun. He had a gray woolen scarf pulled down over his hat and knotted beneath his chin, and he had discarded his duster in favor of a hiplength sheepskin coat that looked as if it hadn't been cleaned since it was removed from the sheep. "You turn renegade?" His crossed eyes took in the Indian mounted beside me.

I assured him that I hadn't, and introduced Rocking Wolf. The bounty hunter laughed shortly and spoke over his shoulder to the half-breed. "Two Sisters' nephew, Long-bow," he said. "I reckon that makes him your cousin. Ain't you going to say howdy?"

Longbow said nothing. He eyed the Indian from beneath the brim of his hat, the whites glistening against the dusky hue of his face.

A gray enamel coffee pot gurgled atop the fire behind Church. "Coffee smells good," I said. "Mind if I have a cup?" I placed my hands on the pommel of my saddle, preparing to dismount. Church raised the gun.

"I'd rather you didn't," he said.

I relaxed my grip on the pommel. On the other side of the fire, Junior gasped and arched his back beneath the blankets that enveloped him, cursing rapidly in a breathless voice. His father placed a gnarled hand against his chest when he tried to sit up and eased him back down. The young man's face shone with sweat in spite of the near-zero weather. There was pink froth on his lips.

I watched him until the convulsions subsided, then returned my attention to the bounty hunter. "Like to tell me what happened?"

"Not especially."

"I'll tell you what happened." The old man spoke without looking up. He was supporting his son's head with his right hand and massaging his chest with the left. His voice was shrill and cracked. "That injun-scalpin' bastard kilt my boy."

"You found him?" Rocking Wolf leaned forward eagerly.

"We found him," said Church, loosening a little. "He

was gutting a buck in a stand of pine eight, ten miles east of here." He snorted. "They told me he was big; they didn't say he was huge. His hand just about swallowed up the bowie knife he was using. We rode right up to him, got the drop on him. I told him to stand up. At first he acted like he didn't hear me. I said it again, and that's when he cut loose.

"He had a rifle inside that carcass. He fired twice, blasting a hole through the back and hitting Junior in the belly with the first shot. There was so much blood and meat splattered over him you couldn't tell which was his and which was the deer's. The second shot went wide. I fired back and so did the breed. I think one of us hit him, because he staggered, but in the confusion he got to his horse and hightailed it east."

"You didn't follow him?" I prodded.

"Hell, no. He knows this country better'n anybody. We'd of rid straight into an ambush. Longbow says he'll return to the trail on the other side of the mountain. We'll head him off from this direction after we break camp. We been riding most of the night."

"What about young Strakey?"

"He's done for. I'd of put him out of his misery hours ago, but the old man won't let me." He grinned spasmodically. "I care about the men I ride with."

"Christ, that's touching."

The mirth fled Church's face. "What's your business here, anyway? Sheriff Goodnight said you was taking a prisoner up to the capital. That him?" He flicked his gun barrel toward the Indian.

I told him about Brainard and about how I came to be riding with Rocking Wolf, including the deal I'd made with his uncle. It was surprising how little time it took to recount the story.

"I don't believe it." This time it was Longbow who

spoke. "Two Sisters hates the white man. He wouldn't drink out of the same lake." The way he said it left me with few illusions regarding his own sympathies in that direction.

"That sounds strange coming from a half-breed who claims to be his son," I retorted.

"Son of a bitch!" he spat, and fired the Dance straight at my head. But by that time I was already moving, flinging myself sideways off the saddle just as the bullet clipped the brim of my hat. I hit the ground, rolled, and came up on the other side of my horse. Longbow drew down on me again.

"Stop."

Rocking Wolf's command, delivered in a dry monotone, made the half-breed pause. He looked up at the Indian. I did too, turning my head just enough to keep both of them in sight.

The Indian had unslung his Winchester, and now he sat with it trained squarely in the center of Ira Longbow's narrow chest. No one, not even Church, had seen him move.

"Ira, you are so damned dumb." The bounty hunter spoke like a father who had caught his son behind the barn with his neighbor's daughter. "Put the gun away before somebody gets killed."

"Tell that to the Indian. My business is with Murdock." He steadied his revolver at my head. I ducked. To hell with my reputation.

"Homer." Church pronounced the name flatly. It was answered by a metallic click from beyond the fire.

The half-breed cast a wary eye in that direction, where the old man, still crouching over his son, had slid the latter's percussion cap pistol from his belt and was pointing it at Longbow. Strakey's white-stubbled jaws worked ruminatively at a plug of tobacco the size of a crabapple.

"I don't like to get mixed up in family quarrels, Ira,"

said Church, "but if you don't put that gun where it belongs, I'll have Homer splatter your brains all over this side of the mountain."

Not too far away, a squirrel leaped down from a tree and thumped through the snow to another, stopping once to chatter angrily at the intruders in its midst. It might have been the most important thing there, the way all of us appeared to be listening to it. Finally, Longbow eased the Dance's hammer back into place and returned it to its holster with a brutal thrust.

"Good boy," said Church. He returned his attention to Rocking Wolf. "Your turn, injun."

The nephew of the chief of the Flathead nation didn't have to be told that two guns were better than one. Without removing his eyes from the half-breed, he uncocked the rifle and slung it back over his shoulder. His face remained impassive as ever. I exhaled, only then realizing that I'd been holding my breath.

"I just give you your life, Murdock," said the bounty hunter. "I hope you remember that."

"What makes you so generous?" I reached up and took hold of the chestnut's bridle, stroking its neck with the other hand to calm it down. Unarmed as I was, it seemed a good idea to keep the animal between me and the half-breed as much as possible.

Church holstered his weapon with a dime-novel flourish, proving that there's a little Henry Goodnight in all of us. "I got one rule," he replied. "I never kill law. Not unless it gets in my way so bad I can't go around it."

"I'd say I'm in your way right now. We're both after Bear Anderson. We can't both have him."

"You ain't in my way. Not yet."

"But if I should be later?"

"Like I said, I hope you remember that I give you your life once." He shot a glance over his shoulder at Longbow,

who stood glaring at us from his side of the fire. "You'd
best ride. I don't know how long I can hold back the breed.
If you get kilt, I'll have to kill the injun too, and I'd rather
not make an enemy of the Flatheads this early in the
hunt."

"I guess that means we don't get any coffee."

"You wouldn't appreciate it anyway. Old Man Strakey
can read sign like a Blackfoot, but one thing he can't do is
make coffee."

"One warning." I mounted the mare and looked down
at him. The scarf gave his narrow face an animal cast, like
a cross-eyed fox. "The Flatheads have been trying to get
the drop on Anderson for fifteen years, and all they've gotten for their trouble is the biggest burial ground in the
Northwest. He didn't get his reputation by running away."

"He ain't been wounded before."

"Ever hunt a wounded bear?"

He shrugged. "I ain't taking no more unnecessary
chances. Warrant says dead or alive. I tried it one way.
There ain't but one way left."

"Good luck." I gathered up the reins and began backing
the horse down the trail. Rocking Wolf followed suit.

"Which way you headed?" called Church.

"East."

"You're the one needs the luck."

Once we were out of effective pistol range we turned
around and headed back the way we had come. After we
had gone a mile, I cast a sidelong glance at the chief's
nephew. "You risked a lot back there," I said.

"I had little to lose." He kept his eyes on the trail.

"All the same, I suppose I should thank you. I can't
think why it sticks in my throat."

He met my gaze. "I said before that I am not yet
prepared to see you die."

Paralleling the trail left by Church and his men, we

reached the point around nightfall where they had shot it out with Anderson. The buck carcass was gone—dragged, judging by the marks in the snow, into a thicker grove of trees a hundred yards to the north. In its place lay a shaggy gray hulk stretched on its side, the hole where its throat had been now empty and black with frozen blood. Its fangs were bared in a death's-head grin. "A pack," observed Rocking Wolf, indicating the paw-prints that overlapped each other and obliterated the tracks left by the bounty hunters' horses. "Fifty, perhaps more. They fought over the kill once and will again. By morning the sound of their further fighting will attract more wolves from the lowlands." He scanned the snow-swept countryside as if searching for the beasts. "Tonight one of us will sleep and the other will stand guard."

"Are you volunteering?"

He looked at me, reading my thoughts. "Not necessarily," he said. "You will remember that I sleep lightly."

The tracks of an unshod horse, a big one, led east around the base of the mountain. Rocking Wolf dismounted to inspect one of the dark spots that mottled the snow around them. They were so similar to those that had marked the bounty hunters' trail that I had paid them little attention, assuming them to have been left by young Strakey. But now I noticed that there were more of them farther on, beyond the point where the opponents had separated. They showed black in the light of the rising moon.

"He has been hit," confirmed the Indian, standing. "Much blood has been lost. He is in trouble."

"More than you think." I pointed to the snow at Rocking Wolf's feet, where the track of a large wolf overlapped one of the big horse's hoofprints.

"Perhaps they have grown tired of venison." He mounted and waved me ahead of him down the trail. "There is much moonlight. We will follow for one hour."

I was glad of the excuse to keep moving. With no clouds for insulation, the entire range was laid bare to the elements, rendering useless our heavy clothing and making the snow squeak beneath our horses' footsteps. I rubbed my face at intervals with my gloves to keep the blood circulating, but as soon as I stopped the numbness would creep back in and I'd be forced to do it again. After a while my arms felt like lead. I kept at it, however, driven on by a boyhood memory of a trapper I had once seen in Doc Bernstein's office, a young man who had been found unconscious in the snow on the outskirts of Staghorn. His face had split from exposure and had begun to ooze blood and raw meat through the cracks. It must have been as painful as it looked, because that night he had made his way to his gun and put a bullet through his brain. I rubbed until the skin felt raw and then I went on rubbing.

The trail led down a steep slope on the windward side of the mountain, an irregular incline swept by the wind in some places to bare rock interrupted in the middle by a crevice some twelve feet wide.

"Devil's Crack," I told Rocking Wolf, once we'd stopped to view it from a distance of fifty yards. "Two miles long and a hundred feet deep at its shallowest point. We'd save several hours if we jumped it."

"And if we did not make it across?"

"Then I guess we'd save the rest of our lives."

He grunted distrustfully, but a quick glance around seemed to assure him that there was no place nearby to set up an ambush, so he gathered up his reins and, slapping his stallion smartly on the rump, took off down the slope at a gallop. I did the same, but there was no way the mare could hope to catch up to an animal at least six years her junior, and that was why we were several lengths behind Rocking Wolf when I spotted the thong.

It had originally been covered with snow, but the wind,

its gusts confined to this side of the mountain, had exposed a two-foot length to glisten wetly in the light of the moon where it had been made fast to an upended tooth of shale. It was taunt as a guitar string and raised about a foot and a half above the ground.

I shouted a warning to the Indian and drew back on the reins so hard the chestnut reared onto its haunches and slid on its rump for twenty feet before coming to a stop. I was pitched off and had to grab the thong in both hands to keep from sliding over the edge. I stopped with my boots dangling in mid-air. But it was too late for Rocking Wolf. His horse hit the thong, screamed, and pitched forward onto its chest with an impact that shook the mountain. For a frozen moment, Indian and horse were a tangle of arms and flailing legs, fighting for traction on the icy rock. Then they sailed over the edge of the crevice and into space. The stallion's screams echoed off the walls for an impossible length of time, then ceased abruptly. The wind whistled irreverently in the silence that followed.

It was not a long silence. I was lying stretched out full length on my back, my gloved hands clutching the thong that had just claimed Rocking Wolf's life and saved mine, when I heard a sound like a guitar string being plucked and the thong, weakened when the Indian's horse had struck it, gave away where it had been lashed to the rock. I began sliding.

I was about to go over when a hand grasped my collar, stopping me. Beneath my feet, an outcropping of brittle snow fell apart and sifted down toward the bottom of the crevice. Icy air played over my boots and up inside my pants legs where they hung over the edge. But the grip on my collar held firm and began pulling me backward. Empty space gave way grudgingly to solid ground. In another moment I had gained enough footing to turn over and see my rescuer. In that instant it occurred to me that I might have been better off if I'd fallen, because I found myself staring into the grinning, bearded face of Bear Anderson.

CHAPTER SEVEN

He was even bigger than I remembered. Crouched though he was, one leg thrust out for balance, its mate drawn up beneath him, a massive hand clutching the jagged rock to which the thong had been tied while he maintained his grip on me with the other, he was nearly seven feet of solid muscle without an ounce of suet anywhere. He was made to look even more ponderous by the bearskin he wore poncho-style over a buckskin shirt and pants tucked into the tops of fur boots the size of snowshoes. The eyes beneath the rim of his fur hood were the clear blue of his Scandinavian ancestors', and his features, despite the leathery grain of his complexion, were even and handsome enough to turn the head of a mining camp's most hardened prostitute. His full beard, like his shoulder-length hair, was reddish and streaked with yellow. The only flaw was a jagged patch near the corner of his jaw on the left side where the whiskers grew sparsely over scar tissue—the remnant, I judged, of an old tomahawk wound. But for that, he hadn't changed in fifteen years.

The mystery of where he had come from so quickly was explained by the snow clinging to his shoulders and the front of his bearskin. Lord knew how many hours he had lain there after setting his trap, covered with snow from head to foot, waiting for his pursuers to come along and blunder into it. He had the patience and ruthless cunning of a tracked cougar. He didn't appear to recognize me, but I don't suppose it would have mattered if he had. I was an intruder in his territory and worse, I had been riding with one of his mortal enemies on his own trail. The grin he wore disturbed me. I had a feeling it was the last thing a lot of Indians had seen this side of the happy hunting ground.

I decided to bluff it out. "Long way down," I said, acknowledging his assistance with a nod.

"Goes all the way to the bottom."

A cracker-barrel answer, flat and noncommittal as a storekeeper agreeing that rain was wet. His voice was gentle and curiously high-pitched for a man his size, but held a harsh edge as if he wasn't used to using it. He watched me through unblinking blue eyes.

"I reckon I would have too, if you hadn't happened along," I ventured.

"Reckon."

The conversation was becoming one-sided. I tried to pull myself farther up the slope, but failed to purchase a grip with my gloves on the smooth wet surface of the rock and gave up. My chest and stomach grew numb where I was lying in the snow. I was painfully aware that the scalphunter's fist on my collar was the only thing that stood between me and oblivion, and from the look on his face I gathered that he was debating with himself whether it might be a good idea to let me go. At length he sighed resignedly and pulled me up onto a better footing.

"Thanks," I said, and started to get up.

He didn't reply. Instead he swept a loglike arm around behind me, crushed me to his chest, and with his free hand thrust against my chin began pushing my head backward until my spine quivered like a drawn bow. One of Ezra Wilson's stitches in the back of my head popped audibly.

"What's your name, injun lover?" Anderson demanded, through his teeth. "What you doing in my mountains?"

I couldn't answer. He was holding me so tightly I couldn't breathe and the pressure on my jaw made it impossible for me to form words. Blood pounded in my head.

"Answer me, injun lover!" He increased the pressure.

My lungs screamed for air. I was like a swimmer going down for the last time within sight of a shore full of people; help was only a cry away, but I was unable to ask for it. My spine creaked where he was bending me backward. I fought to retain consciousness. My eyesight shrank to pinpoints of light in a black shroud. Bear Anderson's contorted features faded into insignificance and I felt myself floating away from my body. Then I felt nothing whatsoever.

Half-formed images chased each other endlessly through my head. Now I was suspended in mid-air, my head, arms and legs dangling while some unseen force bore me upward over uneven ground to where the air grew thin and sharp as flying thorns. Next I was lifted even higher and transported from pale moonlight to abysmal darkness, where small furry things with membranous wings fluttered about me, brushing my face with feathery strokes. In the next moment I was pitched like a sack of grain to the earth. After that there was a long stretch of nothing until I awoke with heat on my face.

The first thing I saw when I opened my eyes was flame. I drew back in panic, pain shooting through my abused joints, only to find to my relief that I was lying on my side and looking into nothing more dangerous than a campfire, consuming a small pile of wood a foot in front of my face. Around me, the warm light cast by the fire rippled over stone and splashed weird, writhing shadows over walls and ceiling tinted orange by the glow. Beyond the flame was a black void. I was in a cave or tunnel of some sort, and I was not alone.

In the entrance, two eyes glowed eerily green in the reflected light of the fire. As I watched them a chunk of wood rolled off the top of the pile and crashed into the heart of the flames, sending up a spurt of yellow and illuminating the opening. I found myself staring into a narrow face with a coal-black muzzle and mouth parted to reveal two rows of sharp, curving teeth separated by a dripping tongue. Amber eyes with black slits in their centers studied me as if in fascination. One pointed ear, the muscles of which had been torn in some long-forgotten fight, refused to stand up like its mate, and so hung sullenly almost to the corner of the jaw. Beyond this was a bushy neck, a deep chest tapering to a visible ribcage, and two powerfully bowed forelegs covered with matted gray fur. The wolf was in view but an instant, and then the flare died and only the glowing eyes remained.

There was a roar in the cave. Something buzzed past my right ear. I heard a yelp and then the thudding sound of feet fading into the distance. A thin stream of dust, dislodged from the cave's ceiling, settled onto my head and down inside my collar. I rolled over onto my right side. In the gloom at the back of the cave, Bear Anderson sat upon a flat rock with a Spencer in his hands, a plume of white smoke twisting out of the barrel.

"Just nicked him," he said, more to himself than to me. "That won't make the old bastard any easier to handle after this."

"You talk like you know him," I said. My voice sounded strange in the comparative silence that followed the shot's echo.

"Ought to. Two years ago he and his pack cost me the best horse I ever had. We go back a long way together, Old

Lop Ear and me." He fished a fresh cartridge out of his pants pocket—he had doffed the bearskin—and reloaded, jacking a shell into the chamber to replace the one he had fired. He grunted with the effort. That's when I noticed the dark stain on his buckskin shirt along his left side.

"How bad is it?" I asked, nodding toward the wound.

"Just a graze." He laid the Spencer on the stone floor by his feet and sat gripping his knees in his enormous hands. "Bullet scraped around the ribs and got stuck in back. Can't reach it, but it ain't doing me no harm. I'm letting it bleed out some before I try to dress it. How you feeling?"

"Sore." I placed a tentative fingertip against the back of my head. It still throbbed, but the cut had ceased to bleed a long time ago. I unwound the bandage and cast it into a dark corner of the cave. Cold air stabbed at the wound. "What I'm wondering about is how come I'm still alive."

He grinned, lighting up his end of the cave. "Not because of anything you did," he said. "You should of said something when I asked who you was, Page. I'd of snapped your spine like a chunk of dry firewood if I didn't recollect you at the last minute."

"What was I supposed to do, knock it out in Morse code on your forehead?"

Behind Bear, my chestnut and a rangy dun that stood a good hand higher than the biggest horse I had ever seen began to snort and nicker, straining at the bonds hobbling their forelegs. They had just caught the wolf's scent. Bear made soothing noises deep in his throat and reached out to stroke the dun's muscular breast. "Easy, Pike." He said something to it in a guttural tongue that sounded like Blackfoot.

"Where are we?" I looked around.

He laughed.

"Don't tell me you don't recognize Spirit Peak! Hell, this is where you and me used to cook our rabbits when we was kids. The injuns think this is where all the evil shades meet to plot their wicked deeds. They won't come nowhere near it."

"You live here?"

"Just part of the time. Mostly I like to be where I can keep an eye on what the Flatheads are up to." He studied me curiously. "You going to tell me how come you was riding with Rocking Wolf?"

"Do I have to?"

"Not if you want some fresh air. It's a ten thousand foot drop from here to the bottom of the mountain."

I told him. He listened in silence.

"Got a badge?" he asked, when I had finished.

I flashed the scrap of metal I carried in my breast pocket. He stared at it a long time, but that was just for show. The Bear Anderson I knew had never learned to read. Finally, he nodded and I put it away.

"So that part's true," he said. "How do I know about the rest? You might be in with that bunch that tried to bushwhack me night before last. Come to think on it, you didn't act very surprised when you seen I was wounded." He reached down and scooped the rifle off the floor with a deft movement of his right arm. "Start talking."

"There's not much to talk about. I met them west of here yesterday, if it was yesterday. How long have I been here?"

"Six hours. Two more from Devil's Crack to here. Keep talking."

"Church—that's the leader of the gang that jumped you —is being paid five thousand dollars by the U.S. government to bring you in, dead or alive. It seems you're standing in the way of a treaty with the Flatheads."

He spat. "A treaty with Two Sisters ain't worth belly skins. He'll sign it with one hand and lift your scalp with the other."

"Tell that to Ulysses S. Grant. He's the one who authorized the warrant."

"What business does General Grant have with me?"

"He's not a general any more. He's the President. That is, he was until recently. At any rate, his signature is still good, since he signed it before he left office. Right now I'd say you're just about the most wanted man in the country."

He grimaced suddenly and placed a hand in the area of his left kidney.

"Why don't you let me take a look at that?" I started to get up, and found myself staring down the bore of the Spencer.

"Sit," he said. I sat.

Outside, the wind hooted past the entrance, turning the entire mountain, which I remembered as a network of caves, into a gigantic pipe organ. The fire flared and buckled with the current of air inside our shelter. It was getting colder outside.

"Hand me that sack," said Bear. He indicated a worn gunny sack heaped against the cave wall near where I sat. It was mottled with brownish stains, some old, others fresh and moist. I hefted it and was surprised to find that it didn't weigh much, though it bulged with its contents.

"What's in it?" I undid the knot in the top.

"None of your business. Hand it here."

I ignored his warning tone and looked inside. It was full of scalps.

"Satisfied?" He stretched out an arm as long as my leg

and snatched the bag from my grip. He opened it and began pulling out specimens, which he stretched out on the floor at his feet. The cave filled with the stench of rotting flesh.

When the last of the scalps—there were seven of them— were lying before him, he produced a bowie knife from the sheath at his belt, cut five leather strips from the fringe on his shirt, and knotted them together. This resulted in a thong six feet long, upon which he proceeded to string the scalps.

"What do those do for you?" I was just beginning to get over the shock of that grisly discovery, when I'd been expecting to find food in the sack. Now eating was the farthest thing from my mind.

"You wouldn't understand it." He tied on the last of the scalps and set the knot with his teeth. Then he stood and secured one end of the thong to a jagged crag in the wall nearest him.

"Try me."

"Ammunition." He stepped across to the opposite wall, found a fissure in the granite, and jammed the thong's knotted free end into it. Now the scalps were strung like hideous Christmas cards across the cave. "You'd be surprised what the sight of a dozen or so of them things hanging from your belt will do to a injun when he's all fired up for a fight. I seen them turn tail and run after just one look. Course, they don't get far."

The stench of the bloody relics was getting to the mare, which whinnied shrilly and tossed its head, trying to get its teeth into the hobbles that held it. Bear's dun, however, remained unperturbed; the big horse had found a patch of green moss growing out of a crack in the stone floor and was busy nibbling at it. The scalp-hunter laid a heavy hand on the mare's neck and smoothed back its bristling withers. Immediately it began to breathe more easily. He had a way with animals.

"You eat recent?" he asked me.

My appetite wasn't what it had been before I'd seen his trophies, but I had no wish to starve to death. I shook my head.

"There's a buckskin pouch under them ashes," he said, nodding toward the fire. "Pull it out."

I seized a stick from the fire and stirred the ashes until I encountered a bulky object and worked it out smoking into the open. Although it had probably been dampened and was still covered with what I supposed had once been wet leaves, the buckskin was now dry beneath a coating of soot. I used the stick to push aside the flap. Immediately the aroma of roasted meat enveloped me. Scalps or no scalps, I was suddenly ravenous. But I remembered my manners. I offered Bear the first piece, a leg so tender it fell apart in my hand. He shook his head.

"You eat it," he said. "I swallowed enough rabbit in the last few weeks to sprout my own fur. That's about the only thing that's left after them last three winters. I had my taste all set for some venison, but your friend Church spoiled that in good shape."

"He's no friend of mine." I said it through a mouthful of meat so hot it made my eyes well up. Bear saw my predicament and tossed me a patched-up canteen full of water. I gulped it too fast and nearly choked to death. It was the best I'd felt in days.

"You grow your rabbits juicy up here," I commented, once I'd recovered and was finishing off the meat.

"It's the pouch does that. I learned it from the Blackfeet. The buckskin holds in all them juices you'd lose if you staked it out over the fire in the regular way. If I had me some dried wild onion skins to crumble over it, I'd show you a real meal."

I grunted my understanding. After the events of the past few days, it didn't even seem strange that I was sitting there surrounded by drying scalps at the top of a mountain listening to a recipe for cooking rabbit. It seemed to go with the territory. I flipped away the last of the bones and wiped my hands off on the front of my coat. "Why'd you kill Brainard?"

He had been whetting his knife on his buckskin sleeve, stropping it back and forth like a razor. Now he paused. "What makes you think I done it?"

"He was shot with the same rifle that was used to kill the Indians who were torturing him. And don't tell me you didn't kill *them*; those are their scalps drying on that thong."

"I done what I would for any white man in the same situation." He resumed stropping. "Once I come across a white trapper after the injuns was finished with him. He was hanging from a tree, just like this Brainard, only this one was all red and slippery from head to foot like a skinned rabbit, on account of that's just what they done to him. And he was still moving. I done for him too, but by that time he had went through so much that I don't suppose it mattered to him. This time I got there early enough to make it worth something. I hope I can count on somebody doing the same thing for me when it comes my turn."

"You think it'll come to that?"

"Bound to. I'm slowing down now, else I wouldn't of had to shoot none of them injuns more than once." He waved his knife in the direction of the dangling scalps. "Sooner or later, some young buck is going to get in a lucky shot, and then I'll be meat for Old Lop Ear."

"Why don't you quit?"

"A man does what he's good at." Rising, he returned the knife to its sheath and reached for his bearskin. "It's almost light. Can you saddle up, or do you want me to do it for you?"

"Where are we going?" I gathered my legs beneath me. Pain rocketed up my spine.

"Devil's Crack. I got a scalp waiting for me at the bottom, remember? By the time we get there, there ought to be enough light to risk the ride down." He threw the bearskin on over his shoulders.

"Thanks, but I'd just as soon stay here and wait for you."

He reached down and took hold of my left shoulder in one hand, crushing it. "Bet you won't."

"Why not?" I grunted, through clenched teeth. He was cutting off my circulation.

"You know as well as me that you ain't getting out of these mountains till you finish the job Two Sisters sent you out to do. I'd heaps rather have you in front of me than at my back."

"What about afterwards?"

"Afterwards is afterwards." He squeezed harder. "Can I count on your company?"

"Where's my saddle?" The words came out in a gasp.

The wind had unfurled a tarpaulin of dirty gray between mountains and sky, so low that when we led our horses out of the cave we found ourselves in the very midst of the haze. We descended five hundred feet before we came out of it. Beneath the ceiling, the panorama of the Bitterroot spread out dizzyingly before us, tents of white dotted with black stands of pine, with here and there a shallow depression to mark the frozen surface of a lake. It had just begun to snow again; I watched as the first wave of flakes emerged from the clouds and began its slow descent to the ground ten thousand feet below, like spent grapeshot falling through the trees. The wind shifted constantly, blowing clouds of white powder back and forth across our path. The air was so cold it seared my throat when I inhaled.

Bear's height, together with the size of the horse he was riding, made me feel like a dwarf astride the chestnut as we picked our way single-file down the side of the mountain, me in front. My escort rode with his Spencer across the pommel of his saddle, his buckskin-gloved hands crossed over it and holding the reins. In front of him, a gunny sack hung on either side of the dun from the saddle horn in the middle. One of them held his scalps. I hadn't seen inside the second sack, but I had a pretty good idea of what it contained. I filed this hunch away in my memory for future reference.

We approached the Crack from the northern end, where it leveled out after a steep climb of nearly two hundred feet from its lowest depth. For us, the climb would be twice as dangerous; we were going down, not up.

Halfway down, the mare lost its footing, and I had to haul hard on the reins, pulling it back onto its haunches to keep both of us from tumbling all the way to the bottom. Behind me, Bear halted his mount and waited until I was in control again before continuing. I glanced at him once over my shoulder. Both his and the dun's heads were enveloped in vapor, like gargoyles snorting steam out their nostrils.

The snow at the bottom of the crevice was piled up to the horses' breasts. It struck me that finding Rocking Wolf's body beneath that muck was not going to be an easy task. Not that it mattered, of course; we had all the time in the world.

Noon found us nearly a mile into Devil's Crack, with the snow still falling softly around us. The horses were lathered and wheezing from struggling through the snow; I was about to suggest that we stop and rest when Bear grunted suddenly and thrust a finger the size of an ear of corn out ahead of him. I looked to see where he was pointing. A couple of yards ahead, a horse's foreleg protruded stiffly straight up from the bank of white. Another few seconds and we'd have stumbled over it.

We dismounted, and together we worked feverishly to claw the snow off our find. It was slow going, as the stuff was wet and heavy and we had no shovels to work with. After about twenty minutes we had cleared away enough of it to see that the leg belonged to Rocking Wolf's stallion. It lay twisted half onto its back, its eyes still wide in its final spasm of terror and a froth of blood frozen on its lips. Its back was broken. Now there remained only one corpse to find.

An hour later, we had cleared out a ragged circle ten feet in diameter around the dead horse down to the bare ground, and still there was no sign of Rocking Wolf's body. Bear and I stared at each other over the dead animal. His expression, bewildered at first, slowly grew thoughtful. He looked as if he was about to speak when a voice floated down to us from somewhere far above our heads.

"One for you, white skin!" Carried on the wind, the voice had an unnatural quality, rendering it almost unrecognizable. "Now it becomes my turn."

Rocking Wolf's words echoed along the walls of the crevice until they became part of the wind itself, and then it was impossible to tell where they left off and the gale began.

CHAPTER EIGHT

"What now?" I asked Bear, after the initial shock had worn off. I had to shout to make myself heard over the mounting wind.

"Why ask me? It's you he was talking to!"

Even as he said it, I realized he was right. If Rocking Wolf had suspected I was leading him into a trap before, he was sure of it now.

"Look for his rifle," I said. "It must be here somewhere. If he still had it, we'd both be dead." I began kicking holes in the banks of snow beyond the clearing.

"No time." The scalp-hunter's tone was clipped. "If we're going to be out of here by nightfall, we'd best be heading south, and that's one climb I'm not going to risk after dark."

"Then what?"

"You leave that to me." He mounted the dun.

I had to crane my neck to look up at him, he was that tall and the horse was that big. "I hope you're not planning on heading east around the mountain. Church and his bunch are waiting to bushwhack you on the other side. You and anyone riding with you."

"Figured that. Mount up."

The sun was a bloody gash between the overcast and the horizon when we vaulted out of the Crack at its southern end. No sooner had we emerged than Bear turned his horse's head east.

"Why don't you just shoot yourself in the head and save time?" I exclaimed.

"There ain't nothing west of here but more mountain and blizzards." His beard bristled over his set jaw. "I'd heaps rather take my chances with men."

"You don't know Church."

Travel at night was impossible with the moon obscured by clouds. We made camp at sundown on a shelf of wind-swept rock on what was now the lee side of the mountain, where firewood was nonexistent and we were forced to share a stiff piece of salt pork from my saddlebags, more of the rations I had bought in Staghorn. Staghorn. Right then, it seemed as far away as San Francisco.

"Give me your hands," said Bear, after we'd finished eating.

"Why?"

"Just give them here." He spoke gruffly.

I extended my hands. Something hard and cold snapped shut around each of my wrists. In that instant I realized that my handcuffs were no longer hanging on my belt. Before I could protest, he smacked me in the chest so hard with the flat of his hand that I lost my balance and toppled over onto my back. A leather thong was wound around both my ankles and pulled taut with a jerk that sent pain shooting straight up my legs. It was all over in the space of a few seconds.

"It must be my honest face," I said acidly.

"I ain't survived fifteen years in the high rocks by taking unnecessary chances," he told me. "Keep that buckhide dry or it'll tighten up on you and bust your feet. You got to relieve yourself, roll over to the edge of the shelf and do it. Try not to fall off." He tossed me my blanket.

"What are you going to do?"

"Sleep." He sat down with his back against the mountain and gathered his bearskin around him, his rifle lying across his lap.

"Good," I said. "See if you can get some for me, too."

I did sleep, though fitfully. Several times I opened my eyes to see Bear's bulk against the scarcely lighter background of the mountain, still awake and tossing an occasional rock at the wolves slinking back and forth beneath the shelf. When he struck one, it would yelp and leap to one side, then snarl up at us, its teeth forming a ghastly white semicircle against the black of its body. "Not tonight, you lop-eared son of a bitch," the scalp-hunter muttered once. But all he got in reply was a rippling growl.

That long night bled almost imperceptibly into a bleak and snowy dawn. It had been snowing steadily for twenty-four hours, and now the entire range was a clean chalk sketch on a background of dirty linen. First light found us entering a narrow pass between the base of Spirit Peak and a rocky knoll to the south.

"If I were planning to ambush anyone, this is where I'd do it," I told my companion, rubbing my wrists where the handcuffs, now removed, had chafed them during the night.

That had about as much effect on him as dropping a stone down a bottomless well and waiting for the splash, so I let it slide. Being unarmed in the midst of danger creates a strange feeling of detachment anyway; knowing that you can't do anything to defend yourself no matter what the circumstances, you don't care what happens. But the feeling wasn't enough to prevent me from keeping an eye on the promontories that flanked our path. That detached I wasn't.

I saw the glint while we were riding abreast through a relatively flat section of pass, and was out of my saddle in the same instant. I struck Bear shoulder-first. I had the fleeting impression, as the pain of impact spread through me, that he wasn't going to budge, but then, like a huge tree whose roots have rotted away, he toppled. We hit the ground in a heap.

He made a growling noise and crooked a huge arm around my neck, catching my adam's apple inside his elbow and crushing it. "A gun!" I managed to croak, before my voice was choked off. I pointed to the top of the cliff.

It sank in on him belatedly. Slowly he released his grip. I inhaled in desperation.

Far above us, feeble sunlight painted a pale strip along something long and metallic sticking out from the top of a line of rocks on the north side of the pass. Beyond that, the blur of what was unmistakably a human face showed light against the bare granite.

"I thought you said he didn't have no rifle," said Bear quietly.

"It could be Church."

"That's dandy. Now all's we got to do is figure out which one of them is going to kill us."

"I might be able to get up there if you'll keep him busy down here," I suggested.

"Why don't you keep him busy whilst I go on up?" His tone was suspicious.

"What am I supposed to do, jump up and down and holler? You've got the only gun."

He repeated the growling noise. Twisting to look down at him, I thought I saw his eyes wander toward the gunny sacks tied to the dun's saddle. For a moment it looked as if he might relent. Then he shook his head, as if he had just won a battle with himself. "Go on up," he said. "Stick to the shadow."

"Give me your knife."

He glowered at me for a moment, then passed over the big bowie. "I expect that back afterwards."

"Stick around. Maybe you can take it off my body."

Using the horses for cover, I crept along the base of the knoll until I was in shadow, then took a deep breath and sprinted across to the opposite side of the pass. There, I flattened out against the mountain and waited for the shots. There were none. I looked up. From this angle, the rifle barrel was invisible, if indeed it was still there. I hoped it was. If there was any moving around to be done up there, I wanted to be the one who did it. I shuffled sideways until I came to a spot where some ancient avalanche had piled a makeshift staircase of stones at the base of the mountain and began to climb. After a while I took off my gloves and put them in my pocket to make the job easier.

It grew steeper as I ascended, until I was crawling straight up a vertical wall with only a shallow foothold here and there and an occasional crag over which I could curl my numb fingers. Once my foot slipped and I had to smack the wall hard with the palm of my right hand to keep from plummeting fifty feet to the jagged pile of rocks at the bottom. The hand tingled as I felt around with my foot for support, but not until I came to a ledge deep enough for me to support myself on my elbows did I notice that I had scraped most of the skin off the palm. I decided that if I ever got out of this alive, Judge Blackthorne was going to be slapped with a lot of medical bills.

At length my head drew level with the line of rocks from which the rifle had thrust itself earlier. I cast wary glances to right and left and, finding no one in sight, pulled myself up and over the edge. Then I drew the knife from my boot—the leather-bound handle stung the raw surface of my hand—and crept forward with the remainder of the mountain at my right shoulder.

I came upon him lying on his stomach with a boulder on either side of him and his cheek resting against the stock of a Remington rifle, the barrel protruding out past the rocks. Before he could move, I flung myself full-length on top of him, crooked my left arm around his throat the way Bear had done with me earlier, and placed the point of the bowie against the tender flesh beneath his chin.

"Let go of the rifle!" I commanded.

There was no response, not even a gasp. After a beat I twisted his head so that I could get a look at his face. It was Homer Strakey, Jr., and he was as dead as the stone ledge upon which he was lying.

He was gun-barrel stiff and his flesh was like ice. I got up off him and turned him over with the toe of my boot; it was like rolling a log. His hands were locked tight around the Remington's action. His eyes were wide open. The wound that had killed him—the one Bear had inflicted—was a gaping black hole in his abdomen just above the belt. There was no sign of bleeding on the ledge. He had been dead a long time, and he hadn't been alive when he was put there.

I stepped to the edge of the shelf and waved my arm to get Bear's attention. It worked, because a shot rang out the instant I showed myself and a bullet whanged off the rock just below my left boot. I leaped back away from the edge.

"Are you crazy?" I shouted, once my heart had resumed beating. "It's me!"

"Sorry."

I called to him to come on up. When his enormous face appeared above the rocks some thirty minutes later, I placed the muzzle of the Remington between his eyes.

"Sorry isn't enough," I said.

The hopelessness of his situation was borne in on him slowly. He had his Spencer slung over his left shoulder by its leather strap and both his hands were engaged in maintaining his grip on the slippery rocks. Even a skull as thick as his would have been blasted apart by a bullet from the Remington at that range.

"You told me to keep him busy," he grumbled at length. "How was I to know you'd be damn fool enough to show yourself like that?"

"Why don't you look before you shoot?" I demanded. "I'd be just as dead whether you meant it for me or not."

"If I was out to kill you, you'd be dead. I don't miss no shot like that."

"Then you knew it was me, damn you!"

"You planning to shoot that, or are you going to talk me to death?"

"I can't." I lowered the rifle, reluctantly. "Firing pin's broken."

"Figured that." He swept the barrel aside with a huge hand and heaved himself up onto the shelf. Standing, he towered over me by nearly a head.

"How?"

"If it wasn't, you'd of shot me the minute I showed. That's the easiest way out of the mess you're in, and if I remember right, you never was one to take the rough road when you didn't have to." He spotted young Strakey's body lying a few feet away beneath a film of freshly fallen snow. "You do that?"

"Not me. You. He was dead when I got here."

He nodded. "That explains the busted firing pin. If this Church is the heller you told me about, he wouldn't go off and leave no working gun with a dead man for anybody to pick up."

"He didn't die here," I said. "There's no blood, and he wasn't strong enough to climb up here without help. Question is, why'd they go to all this trouble?"

"Trying to slow us down, most likely."

"Why, when they could just as well shoot us from ambush?"

He shook his leonine head. "I don't know. I was him, I'd try to hedge my bet, set some sort of trap that can't go wrong. Can't think why he'd pass up a set-up like this." His brow furrowed, and stayed that way for a long moment. Then something dawned over his features. "Unless he thought of a better one." He swung around and took a step toward the edge over which he had just climbed. "Let's ride."

"What's your hurry?"

He didn't reply. He began backing down the way he had come.

"What about him?" I jabbed the barrel of the Remington toward Strakey's body.

He looked at it hard, as if seeing it for the first time. "Pitch him over. Maybe he'll keep Old Lop Ear off our backs for a night."

We put in a lot of saddle time during the next two days. That day we rode until long after dark, camped for six hours, and were moving again before sunup. This time he didn't bother handcuffing me, which I supposed meant something, but I was too exhausted to puzzle it out. Maybe it had something to do with me telling him about the broken firing pin when I might have tried to use the Remington to bluff him out of his own firearm. Whatever his reasons, I had somewhere along the line gained a measure of his trust, which wasn't an easy thing to do.

I had not, however, gained all of it. He wouldn't explain why we were in such a hurry, for instance; when I pressed him, he would give his horse a kick and surge ahead of me until my words were drowned out in the drumming of the dun's hoofs. He spoke rarely, and then only in monosyllables when silence became inconvenient. Snow came in spurts, now light, now so heavy it was impossible to see past the flurry of dollar-sized flakes. By noon of the second day it had let up enough for us to see the cabin huddled against the south face of a lopsided mountain on the western fringe of the Bitterroot.

Even then, it would have been invisible but for a pale gray ribbon of smoke drifting up from the rough stone chimney; wedged into a triangular chink in the mountain itself, the log structure appeared at first glance to be nothing more than a pile of wind-toppled trees. Only upon closer inspection did the semi-symmetrical nature of its construction become apparent. In the spring and summer, it was probably masked by foliage. Now, it was little more than a black strip showing above the banks of snow which were piled up to its single tiny window.

We were perched midway down a slope that graded gently downward before us for another two hundred yards before leveling out in front of the cabin. Bear swung his great head in a slow arc from left to right, noting each detail in the landscape like a minister studying his scripture. Then he hooked the thumb and little finger of his right hand inside his mouth and whistled shrilly. The sound pierced the brittle air and echoed from the mountaintops; from a distance, it might have been a bird calling to its mate.

When perhaps a minute had crawled past without an answer, he whistled again. Again it was met with silence. The horses fidgeted and snorted steam out their nostrils.

"What I was afeared of," said Bear.

No sooner had he said it than the door of the cabin swung open with a bang that reverberated like a pistol shot around the circle of mountains and Church stepped out into the open.

His right arm was locked around the throat of an Indian woman with a shape like a sack of feed. At that distance, her features were a blur, but her complexion, braided hair, and drab costume of skins left no question about her race. In his left hand, the bounty hunter gripped his Navy Colt with the barrel buried in the folds of her stout neck.

"You got yourself a brave squaw, Anderson!" He shouted twice as loud as he had to, to make himself heard. The mountains rang with his nasal tenor. "She'd of let me bust her arm before she whistled back. I'm kind of glad she didn't, though. I like this way better."

"Your squaw?" I queried, out of the corner of my mouth.

Bear nodded. "Bought her off a Blackfoot sub-chief from the plains, along with a hunnert pounds of cracked corn for Pike, here. He wouldn't make the deal unless she went with it."

"What's it going to be, Anderson?" shouted Church. "Do you come in guns down, or do I make a mess right here in front of your cabin?"

"You're too late, Church!" I called out. "This man's in my custody."

Bear glanced at me suspiciously. I ignored it.

"That you, Murdock?" called the bounty hunter.

I told him it was.

"I can't see your badge from here. You might be an accomplice pulling my leg. Not knowing any better, I might accidentally blow your head off."

"How bad do you want her back?" I asked Bear.

"She's an awful good cook."

"I was afraid you'd say something like that. Stall him."

The scalp-hunter raised his voice. "How much time I got to think about it?"

"Don't care for her much, do you?" It was a threat.

"I'm tired, damn it! Give me time!"

Church squinted toward the pale glimmering of light beyond the clouds. "One hour," he said. "You better come up with the right answer, though. One more dead injun won't mean much in this part of the country." His arm still around the woman, he backed into the cabin and slammed the door.

We retreated up the slope into the cover of a stand of skeletal maple trees and dismounted.

"Is that your cabin?" I asked my companion.

"Built it two years ago. Ain't four people in the whole range know about it besides me and Little Tree, there, and all of them's Blackfoot."

"How'd Church find out about it?"

He shrugged his massive shoulders. "Nothing's secret if more than one knows about it. Old White Mane hunts these parts all year long; he'd sell out his tribe for a bottle of good whiskey. Anyhow, it don't matter how they found out. I expected something like this when I seen that dead man they left behind to slow us down. I said before that Church was the kind that likes to make sure nothing goes wrong." He rubbed a thumb thoughtfully along the scarred portion of his jaw. "How soon can you get around behind that cabin?"

"What behind? There isn't any behind. You built the damn thing right into the mountain!"

"You climb good. You proved that back at the pass."

I searched his face for some sign of deceit. I found none. "You're getting awfully trusting suddenly," I said. "Back at the pass you didn't want me out of your sight."

He grunted. "You can move without being seen. They'd spot me a mile away."

"Church is no fool. It'll be guarded."

"I didn't say it'd be easy."

"What do I do once I get there?"

He untied one of the gunny sacks from the horn of his saddle—the one without the scalps—and set it on the ground. Reaching inside, he drew out a kerosene lantern of rusted metal and glass. "As soon as you get up on top of the roof, I want you to chuck this down the chimney." He held it out for me to take. Liquid sloshed around inside the base.

"Are you serious? That'll go off like dynamite! What about your squaw?"

"She'll be outside when you do it. Just wait for my signal." He jiggled the lantern impatiently. I took it.

"How about giving me the rest of what's in that sack?" I asked him.

He started as if struck in the face. "What you talking about?"

I nodded toward the sack, which he had been in the act of tying back onto his saddle. "There's a .45 caliber Deane-Adams five-shot revolver in that bundle. Leslie Brainard took it off me and you took it off the Indians who got it from him. There was a rifle too, a Winchester, but you don't have that. Likely he threw it away after emptying it at the Indians. What I'm interested in right now is the revolver. How about it? You're going to be in need of another gun hand when the shooting starts."

"Why should I trust you with a gun when I didn't trust you with my knife? You never gave that back, come to think on it."

"I didn't stick it into your ribs either. That should prove something."

He dipped into the sack without another word and handed me the holster and gun. I strapped it on, drew the revolver, and spun the cylinder to make sure it was loaded.

It wasn't. Grinning at him, I loaded it from the supply of shells on the belt. "You don't miss a trick, do you?"

"Just don't get no ideas about using it on me," he warned. "That's been tried before."

I gave him a mock salute and moved off in a crouch through the trees.

"One thing." Bear's low murmur crackled in the crisp air.

I stopped and looked back at him. In his shaggy bearskin he resembled a hoary old oak standing among the anemic maples.

"Underneath all that snow there's an inch of dried acorns on the roof. I put them there last summer to let me know if some injun was trying what you're about to."

"Is that all?" I snapped. "What about a moat and crocodiles?"

"Nope. Just acorns."

It took me the better part of our allotted hour to circle around to where the cabin was socked away in the mountain's broad base; brush being scarce, I had to take advantage of intermittent fierce squalls of snow in order to dash from one scrub patch to another, a clear enough target for anyone watching closely through the window. I hoped that whoever was manning that station was too busy rubbing the frost off the glass to spot me during those brief periods. Fortunately, that seemed to be the case, because by the end of the hour I was scaling the craggy surface of the rock toward the snow-covered cabin roof, and there were no holes in me.

My relief was short-lived. I was six feet off the ground when a gun was cocked loudly behind me and Ira Longbow offered me the choice of either coming back down or taking a bullet in the back of the head. I chose the former.

CHAPTER NINE

I glanced back over my shoulder. He was standing a couple of yards back from the rock wall, Dance in hand. His tracks in the snow indicated that he'd just come around from the other side of the cabin, where he had undoubtedly been watching my approach.

"Who says lawmen are dumb?" he said approvingly as I began my descent. "You know, I'd of killed you right where you was if Church wasn't so soft on that badge. I think he'd like to wear one hisself. Drop the gun."

I was still hanging on with both hands. Balancing myself precariously, I reached back with two fingers and flipped the revolver out of its holster. It landed in the snow with a muffled thump.

"That's real good. Down, boy."

The snow was slippery where I'd trampled it while searching for my first foothold on the way up. I tested it carefully with one foot before I let all my weight down on the ground. Then I slipped.

Longbow reacted as I'd hoped he would. Faced with a similar situation, a professional would have stepped back out of the danger zone; not the half-breed. He lunged forward, thrusting the barrel of the six-shooter at me. I tucked his outstretched arm beneath my right armpit and twisted left, grasping his wrist in my free hand as I did so. This accomplished two things: First, it jarred the bone of his wrist against my left hipbone, making him release the gun; second, it allowed me to throw all my weight onto my right leg and fling him, head first, into the stone wall down which I'd just climbed. He folded into a heap at the base of the wall.

Time was running out. In another minute Church would emerge from the cabin to learn Bear's answer to his ultimatum; I was fairly sure he hadn't heard the commotion over the whistling of the wind about the structure's thick walls, but I couldn't afford to have him find me there, not when he had the Indian woman for a shield and another man with a gun inside. If Old Man Strakey hadn't been armed before, he certainly was now that his son had no further use for the percussion cap pistol he'd been carrying. I located my gun and, after knocking snow out of the barrel, put it in its holster. Then I dragged Longbow's unconscious form around the curve of the mountain, threw snow over it, and did what I could to smooth over the tracks on my way back. I was counting on the bounty hunter being too busy watching the top of the slope to notice the footprints that remained. Deciding not to try and find the Dance in the snowbank where it had fallen, I began climbing the wall once again.

I had just cleared the corner of the roof and was still moving when Church came out dragging Little Tree. I held my breath. Hanging by both hands, I was unable to get to my gun. If he looked up I was dead.

But he didn't look up. His attention was centered on the stand of maples at the top of the slope. I continued my upward progress.

"Time's up, Anderson!" he shouted. "What's your answer?"

Seconds ticked by, during which I placed my feet carefully in each foothold lest he hear the noise in the overpowering silence that followed his call. Even the wind had died. He cocked the Colt with a dry click. The woman gasped. Anderson had appeared atop the slope.

I stepped down onto the roof, first one foot, then the other. Beneath twelve inches of snow there was a muffled crunch as I released my hold on the mountain. I froze. Church didn't turn. Slowly I removed the lantern from my right shoulder, over which I had slung it by its metal bail.

"Don't shoot!" Bear's strident voice, so high-pitched for a man his size, echoed throughout the clearing. "I'm coming in."

Church made a sound of satisfaction deep in his throat. "Now you're getting smart! All right, get rid of that rifle and come in slow. Remember, I got two men inside the cabin with guns."

That was a bluff. He was keeping Ira Longbow as his ace in the hole.

Bear hurled the Spencer out ahead of him. It executed three complete spins and landed butt-first in the snow, its barrel pointing skyward. He gave his horse a gentle kick and the two of them moved forward down the slope.

The chimney was a column of soot-blackened stones sticking two feet up out of the snow on the opposite corner of the roof. I made my way over to it, stepping carefully on the layer of acorns beneath the snow. My pants legs were soaked above the tops of my boots.

"Hold it!" roared the bounty hunter. I stopped, reaching toward my gun. "Where's Murdock?"

There was a tense moment while the question repeated itself again and again among the high rocks. Slowly, Church's head began to turn.

"Ira?" For the first time since I had met him, the arrogance was missing from his tone. Half-formed fear played about the edges.

A hundred yards beyond the cabin, Bear raised his right

arm above his head and brought it down with a savage slic-
ing motion. It was the signal.

I lifted the lantern high over the smoking chimney and
heaved it down through the opening. It struck bottom with
a crash. I leaped back in the same instant, but not in time
to avoid singeing my eyebrows in the jet of flames that
erupted up out of the chimney.

Someone screamed inside the cabin. By that time
Church had already swung about, his arm still around the
woman, gun barrel rotating in search of a target. I
launched myself from the roof and came down on top of
both of them. The squaw squirmed free.

The bounty hunter and I grappled in the snow, rolling
over and over as he tried to maneuver his Colt into firing
position. Both my hands were locked around his wrist, but
it didn't budge. He had the wiry strength of a mountain
lion. His other hand closed around my throat in a death-
grip. The blood pounded in my broken head. Finally I let
go of his wrist with my right hand and clouted him on the
chin, once, twice. The gun dropped from his hand.

The cabin door banged open and a human pillar of
flame ran bellowing out into the open. It was Homer
Strakey, Sr., ablaze from head to foot. He fell headlong
into the snow and began rolling, shrieking incoherently
and slapping at the flames that engulfed him.

I was getting up off the stunned Church when something hard and cold was pressed against the base of my
skull and I heard a deep, fury-wracked voice at my ear.
"This is where you finish up, Murdock!"

I didn't stop to think. Dropping to one knee, I swept my
left arm around, catching the arm holding the gun with my
elbow and knocking it to one side. Ira Longbow, his hair
matted on one side and his face streaked with blood from
the cut I'd opened on his head earlier, stumbled backward,
reeling to catch his balance. He succeeded, and brought

the Dance around to fire. At the same time, I reached for my own gun. A crawling sensation took hold of my insides. My holster was empty.

The Deane-Adams lay in the snow between us where it had fallen when I'd left the roof. There was a pause while the half-breed came to realize the superiority of his position. Behind him, the window and open door of the cabin blazed brightly; against that background, the leer that came over his lean features was diabolic. His finger tightened on the trigger.

The air throbbed with a sudden explosion. The whole right side of Longbow's face burst open and his head spun halfway around on his neck. His gun flipped from his hand, he pirouetted on his left foot, and crumpled into the cinder-blackened snow. After a few kicks he lay there without moving, eyes and mouth wide open, the good side of his face turned as though looking back at me over his shoulder. The sound of the fire greedily devouring the log cabin dominated the scene.

I turned. Fifty yards up the slope, Bear Anderson lay on his stomach in the snow where he had dived when the action started, his Spencer braced against his right shoulder and supported on his elbows. The echo of his shot could still be heard receding into the distance.

He couldn't have thrown the rifle into a more convenient spot if he'd been practicing for a week. It had been no accident; he hadn't survived a decade and a half of Flathead enmity by leaving things to chance. It was no wonder that the Indian women regarded him as the embodiment of the evil spirit.

Church was beginning to stir. I picked up my gun and got hold of his Navy Colt before he could retrieve it. He cursed, spat out what looked like a piece of a tooth, and climbed unsteadily to his feet. "Goddamn you, Murdock."

"It wouldn't surprise me if He did." I returned my gun

to its holster and stuck the Colt inside my belt. Then I stood back. "Get going."

The bounty hunter remained motionless, eyeing me suspiciously.

"What in *hell* do you think you're doing?" Bear approached on foot, leading his horse and carrying the Spencer.

Near the burning cabin, Little Tree had gotten up out of the snow and was watching the scene with glittering black eyes. Her face, although round, was smooth and unwrinkled and somewhat pleasant. Her ordeal hadn't seemed to upset her as much as might be expected, but then she was living with the most dangerous man in the Northwest and was probably used to such conditions.

"Now we're even," I told Church. "Pick up your friend and go."

"What about my gun?" he asked.

"I'm fair," I said. "I'm not stupid. You need something to shoot game, you've got Strakey's pistol."

He stood his ground a moment longer, watching me, or so I thought, in his cockeyed fashion. Then he nodded. "We left our horses on the other side of the mountain." He turned to see to his partner.

Old man Strakey's hands and face had gotten the worst of the burning; blisters the size of Michigan cherries were beginning to swell on the skin. But he got up with Church's help and staggered off supported by the bounty hunter, his tattered clothes still smoking. When their backs were turned, Bear raised his rifle and sighted down the barrel. I grabbed it and pushed it away. The scalphunter glared and made as if to strike me with the butt, only to check the motion when he found himself staring down the bore of my revolver.

"I've got this jackass sense of honor that will probably

get me killed someday," I explained. "But he handed me my life once, and now I'm returning the favor."

"I'm obliged, Murdock." Church had stopped just past the corner of the cabin, now a flaming shell, to look back. Despite his lack of size, he appeared to have no difficulty supporting his companion's bulk. "It won't get you no prizes, though," he added. "Now I only got to split that five thousand two ways."

Bear was forced to watch them leave while I kept him covered. When they were out of sight and my gun had been put away, he turned to the woman and barked at her in rapid Blackfoot. She replied softly in the same tongue. He nodded once, curtly.

"Let's ride," he said.

"Where to?" I asked.

"There's a Blackfoot village a day's ride west of here, in the plains. I'm going to leave Little Tree with her own peo ple until this is over. Which it would of been but for you."

He had his foot in the stirrup and was about to mount the dun when he arched his back suddenly and toppled backward seven feet to the ground, where he lay as life-lessly as Ira Longbow's mutilated corpse.

CHAPTER TEN

The heat of the fire was terrific on the back of my neck as I loosened the rough woolen scarf that enveloped Bear's throat beneath the collar of the bearskin. His great chest swelled with his first unfettered breath, then relaxed as he exhaled mightily. His face was flushed and slick with perspiration. He blinked and looked at me.

"What happened?"

"That's my question," I said.

"Don't know. Everything went gray and I felt myself going over." He gritted his teeth and grunted as if undertaking some superhuman effort, but succeeded only in lifting his head a fraction of an inch up out of the snow. Gasping, he let it drop back. "I can't move."

I prodded his slablike ribcage with my fist. "Feel that?"

"No."

"How about this?" I smacked his left thigh with the flat of my hand.

He shook his head.

"Try lifting your hands."

His right hand came up readily. Its mate remained still at his side. Something glimmered in his clear blue eyes. Fear?

I looked at Little Tree, who had knelt in the snow on the other side of him. "Do you speak English?"

"Some little." Her voice was soft, almost inaudible.

"Help me get him into the shelter of that rock." I jerked

my head in the direction of the mountain, where internal stresses had long ago thrust a broken shard of rock several yards square away from the mountain so that it formed an awning four feet above the ground.

We were half an hour pulling and shoving Bear's three hundred and fifty pounds through the snow to where the sloping shelf formed a bulwark against the elements. That done, I directed the squaw to fetch my horse from among the maples at the top of the slope where I had tethered it. "We'll stay here for tonight," I told Bear, once I'd caught my breath. "Tomorrow we start for Staghorn."

"We will like hell!" Again he tried to get up, with the same results. He fell back panting.

"That bullet you picked up is a lot deeper than you let on," I said. "The same thing happened to the captain of my outfit at Gettysburg. He had a ball from a Confederate rifle pressing against his spine, paralyzing him. Your lead must have just shifted. If it shifts back in the right direction, you might be able to move again."

"And if it don't?"

"It will probably kill you."

"Can't you get it out?"

"I'm not even going to try. If I made a mistake, I'd either kill you or paralyze you for life. I've got to get you to a doctor."

He snorted. "Why bother? Me dying is the only way you're going to get back to town with your scalp."

"That wouldn't say much for me, would it? You've saved my hide twice."

"I reckon you was right," he said, after a pause.

"About what?"

"About that honor of yours getting you killed."

"Staghorn's only a couple of days' ride from here," I

said, ignoring the remark. "What they've got for a doctor is
worse than no doctor at all, but if I can get you to town I
may be able to send for one that can do some good."

"No go Staghorn," said Little Tree.

I looked up. She had finished tethering my mare to a
stripling that grew flush with the wall of the mountain and
was standing just beyond the shelf with her fists clenched
at her sides. Her expression was wooden.

"Why not?" I asked.

"Bear hang."

"How did you find out about that?"

She shrugged. "White man's way. Kill men, white man
hang. No go Staghorn."

"We don't know that he'll hang," I said, and looked at
Bear. "It's your decision. You can either go to town and
take your chances with the law or stay here and wait for
Church."

"Some choice," he growled.

"Sorry, but I don't have anything better to offer."

"Go Blackfoot village," said Little Tree. "Medicine man
there."

I shook my head. "I have nothing against your beliefs,
but no amount of wailing and shaking of rattles is going to
get that bullet out of his back. It's Staghorn or nowhere."

"How you going to get me over the mountains?" chal-
lenged the scalp-hunter. "I don't roll easy."

"We can fix up a litter."

"What you mean 'we'?"

"Little Tree and I. Don't say she's not going; there's a
blizzard coming, and it's been too long since I rode the Bitterroot regularly for me to attack it in weather like that
without a guide. You'd be no help at all in your condition.
If you decide to go, she's coming along."

He didn't like it, but there was no fighting my logic. "Ain't you afeared all that moving might shove the bullet the wrong way?" he said, after a moment.

"It's a chance we have to take. But I wouldn't worry too much about it. If it were going to shift that easily, it probably would have while we were moving you just now."

His brow darkened. "Then why in hell did you do it?"

At that moment, the entire front of the blazing cabin collapsed with a resounding *frump*, sending fiery logs rolling and skidding across the snow. Now the structure was nothing more than a pile of burning timber with a stone chimney rising naked from one corner.

"Would you rather we left you there to fry?" I asked him.

He appeared to think things over. Finally he said, "You might as well go ahead and build the litter. We won't live to see morning anyway."

"What's that supposed to mean?"

His eyes slid past my shoulder. I turned to follow his gaze. At the top of the slope, dozens of sleek gray forms milled about among the bare maples, sniffing the ground from time to time and exposing lolling red tongues to the frigid air. There were more than a hundred of them. One, a big monster with a shaggy mane and a dangling ear, stood partway down the grade with its legs straddling our trail, staring at the smoldering wreckage of the cabin as if mesmerized by the flames.

"Didn't take them as long to finish off that dead bounty hunter as I figured," Bear said.

I gave Little Tree the bowie knife and instructed her to cut some brush for a windbreak while I disposed of Ira Longbow's body in a snowbank as far away from the shelter as possible. On her way to the scrub, the squaw picked up the Spencer from the ground where Bear had dropped it

when he fell and took it along for protection from the
wolves. I swept up Longbow's revolver and stuck it into my
belt beside Church's Colt. All told, and assuming that Bear
had enough ammunition on him for another full load, I es-
timated we had approximately forty rounds among us. If
the woman and I were lucky enough to down an animal
with each shot, that left us with only about sixty wolves to
deal with. What was I worrying about?

That afternoon we built a fire using sticks of unburned
wood from the ruins of the cabin and left an opening a
foot wide in the windbreak for the smoke to escape. Over it
Little Tree cooked a neck of venison that she had rescued
from a small storage cellar beneath the wreckage—we had
no time for Bear's special method of roasting—and after-
ward we ate in silence while snow piled up outside the shelter. I thought that if this weather continued, most of the
mountain passes would soon be blocked, and wondered if
perhaps the Flatheads weren't already on their way to the
plains to winter and make plans for the spring uprising,
new moon or no. I didn't dwell on it. I had enough to oc-
cupy my mind without wasting time on something over
which I had no control.

I used what brush I could rustle up to construct a litter,
bound together with the last of the fringe from Bear's
buckskin shirt. When it was finished it didn't look as if it
would support his tremendous weight, but it was the best I
could manage without access to the maples atop the ridge,
where the wolves had bedded down to wait out the remaining daylight. We'd find out for sure tomorrow—if any of us
lived that long.

Night settled like lampblack over the mountains. Bear
slept quietly beneath his blanket, Little Tree beside him
wrapped in mine, while I took the first watch at the opening. I had the scalp-hunter's Spencer across my lap.

The warmth inside the shelter with the fire going made me drowsy. More than once I caught myself just before my chin hit my chest and was forced to scrub my face with handfuls of snow taken from outside the opening to wake up. After a while, though, even that became useless, and I dozed off around ten.

I awoke to find the fire guttering among chunks of glowing charcoal and the snow in front of the shelter alive with wolves. Then I realized that it had been the horses' frantic neighing that had awakened me. I started involuntarily. The movement startled a big male that had been sniffing curiously at the windbreak into going for my right hand. I jerked it back. The wolf's jaws closed over empty air with a snap. Before it could react, I swung the Spencer around and caught it on the end of the snout with the butt. It yelped in rage and pain and lunged forward through the opening, jaws working like a sewing machine.

Its breath was hot and rank on my face when I swung the rifle back the other way, thrust the muzzle into the thick fur at the animal's throat, and pulled the trigger. The air exploded inside the shelter. Blood and meat and tufts of fur flew all over. The wolf slumped over me heavily, its jaws still agape, eyes wide open and glassy.

Bear and the woman were awake—what else could they be?—but if they were talking I couldn't hear them, because my ears were still ringing from the blast. My clothes were slimy with blood from my collar to the tops of my boots. Bits of fur floated down all around me. The air stank of cordite and something else just as strong. Burning hair. I looked down and saw that the animal's coat was smoldering where its hindquarters had come to rest in the middle of the dying fire. Using both hands, I rolled the limp body off my legs and with some effort succeeded in pushing it out through the opening with my feet. Immediately it was fallen upon by its fellows, who tore at it and dragged it away, fighting over it among themselves. In the center of the melee, the rangy male with one limp ear lunged this way and that, drawing blood from flanks and shoulders until order was restored. Then, holding the pack at bay with threatening snarls, it stepped forward and helped itself to the bounty. At length some of the others joined in cautiously, but the majority was left to pace restlessly back and forth and watch the proceedings with twitching tails and murder in their eyes. In no time at all there was nothing left of the corpse but bones and hair.

Little Tree insisted upon helping me off with my coat and pants, and while I huddled next to the rebuilt fire wrapped in the blanket she had just relinquished, scrubbed them in the snow outside the opening to remove the worst of the blood. The wolves, their appetites sated temporarily, eyed her from a safe distance beyond reach of the flames. Their eyes glittered greenly from time to time in the reflected firelight. When she was finished she hung the garments from the windbreak to dry.

"Now we got one less cartridge than we had before," Bear said. He was staring up at the stone ceiling, snug beneath his coarse-woven Indian blanket. His voice came faintly, as if from a long way off; the whining noise in my ears had only just begun to fade.

"What should I have done? Strangle him?"

"You got my knife, ain't you?"

I reached down to feel the hilt of the bowie in the top of my right boot, where I had stuck it after Little Tree had returned it to me. "I never thought about it," I admitted. "Much as I'd have liked to try my hand at killing a full-grown timber wolf with a knife while it was gnawing happily away at my throat. Especially after that same knife had been used to cut brush."

He had no answer for that. Or, if he had, he kept it to himself. In any case he did not pursue the point.

"I see to horses," said Little Tree. She picked up the Spencer and stepped out through the opening.

There was silence inside the shelter after that, while Bear and I listened to the wind whistle past the opening. It gusted at intervals, hooting gleefully as it buckled the fragile walls of the enclosure and blew smoke into our faces. Razor-edged blasts spat bits of snow through chinks in the windbreak.

"I fell asleep," I said.

"Figured that," Bear replied.

"I figured you did. That's why I admitted it."

The squaw returned. "Horses all right. I watch now. You sleep."

I was in no mood to argue. My head was throbbing and I was tired of propping my eyelids open with my thumbs. I drew the blanket up to my chin and stretched out beside the fire. I was asleep before my head hit the floor of the shelter, which was merciful, because it was frozen hard as rock.

The blizzard was upon us in full force when we broke camp the next morning. Wind roared past our ears, whipped stinging grains of ice like bits of ground glass into our faces, whited out the landscape until it was impossible to sort out earth from sky. Under such conditions, I was glad I'd held firm on the subject of Little Tree going along to act as guide. She would ride the mare while I hauled her mate behind the big dun.

Although the litter creaked beneath Bear's weight when we lifted one end of it, it proved strong enough to support him, and once I had flattened the ends of the wooden supports with the blade of the bowie to form runners, the entire burden slid across the surface of the snow as easily as any sled. I secured the litter with a thong to the scalp-hunter's saddle so that it dragged behind the dun, and mounted gingerly, the way any experienced rider does when stepping into a strange pair of stirrups. The big horse fidgeted beneath the rig and the unfamiliar weight on its back, but at a word from its prostrate master it adjusted itself grudgingly to the situation. I stroked its sleek mahogany neck to show it who was in command.

"Everything all right back there?" I shouted to Bear, over the howling gale.

"Let's just ride."

We started with a jolt. Leather creaked, limb groaned against green limb, makeshift runners scraped over fresh powder. In our wake rode Little Tree to keep an eye on our progress. I cast a glance back in her direction. Beyond her, vague gray shapes bounded through the flying snow toward the bank in which I had buried Ira Longbow. They swarmed over it, digging with all four paws. Soon, however, even that scene was lost amid the swirling particles of white.

CHAPTER ELEVEN

We were crossing over old ground in the beginning, but if we hadn't known what direction we were going, none of us would have realized it. What had been hills of snow were now sinkholes, hollowed out by the wind, while level spots through which Bear and I had passed without hindrance a few days earlier were heaped as high as ten feet. Whole stands of pine and maple had been all but obliterated; in other places they had been swept clean where before only their pointed tops had shown. What landmarks remained were blurred behind drifting clouds of white powder so that they resembled features in a grainy tintype.

The wind was tearing out of the east at between forty and fifty miles per hour. I had my kerchief tied over the lower part of my face as feeble protection against frostbite, while Little Tree rode with her chin huddled in the collar of her fur-faced cowhide jacket, one of a handful of items she had been able to salvage from the unburned cellar of the cabin. Bear, the most likely candidate for death by freezing due to his immobile state, was wrapped from head to foot in every available blanket. But for the snow, we might have been veiled mourners transporting the mummified remains of our king to a tomb on the banks of the Nile.

What was two days' ride for a man alone on horseback was considerably more for a man and a woman hauling a litter through one of the worst blizzards on record. Missing Devil's Crack cost us a full thirty-six hours. Most of the passes being closed to us, we were forced to rely on mountain trails and narrow clefts in the high rocks, some of them so cramped we had to dismount and walk our horses single file, Little Tree leading the mare by its bridle, me driving the big dun from behind as if it were an ox plowing a field. At these times we stopped often to disengage the broad litter where it had wedged itself between the rocks. In three days we made barely twenty miles.

I had been wrong when I'd told Bear not to worry about the bullet in his back shifting while he was being moved. At intervals his paralysis gave way to agony as the lead wobbled about next to his spinal column, relieving his numbness just long enough for the pain to set in. Although he bore it without complaint, his suffering was evident in his features. That's the essential difference between man and beast. I'd have shot a dog before letting it go through the hell he accepted as a matter of course.

We were emerging from one of these clefts on a downhill grade toward the close of the third day when I stopped short and signaled the squaw, who was walking behind me, to draw back from the opening. A hundred yards beyond, the entire Flathead nation was pouring onto the circular plateau below us from a forest to the east. At its head rode Chief Two Sisters.

He wore a white woven coat decorated with broad bands of green—the labor, most likely, of the squaw of some ambitious brave. His tarnished-silver hair was braided in front, loose in back, and bound with ornaments bearing the Salish symbols of strength and virility. In the waning light, his face was old and drawn but hard, the eyes sunken beneath his square, jutting brow, mouth turned downward into a permanent scowl. He shifted uncomfortably from time to time on his horse's back, but I gathered that this was not so much from pain as from discomfort caused by

the strip of deerhide that was wound tightly around his injured ribcage, part of which peeped above the V of his coat
as he leaned over to dig a lump of ice out of the top of his
moccasin boot. Like his braves, he rode with a rifle slung
over his left shoulder. The difference was that, while most
of the others carried single-shot Springfields—the kind the
army had given them several years earlier as a token of
good faith—his was the Henry repeater that had been taken
from me by Rocking Wolf. Apparently he didn't share his
nephew's contempt for the weapon.

At his side rode a muscular-looking individual in a
buffalo robe, the only visible part of his face a narrow strip
of flesh showing between a scarf wrapped around his lower
features and a headdress crowned by a pair of curving
buffalo horns. This had to be the medicine man whose an-
tipathy toward me I had sensed in the chief's lodge something over a lifetime ago. His eyes were hard and shifty,
like those of medicine men everywhere.

I watched from the cover of a vertical pillar of rock
while the mass of warriors, with an occasional feminine
face sprinkled among their numbers, slowed to a halt
behind the chief's raised right hand. Silence prevailed
while Two Sisters scanned his surroundings. His eyes
swung in my direction and I froze, my hand gripping the
butt of the Deane-Adams. But they moved on without
pausing, and when it was apparent that he had satisfied
himself that they were alone on the plateau, the chief
turned and said something to the man mounted at his side.
The wind drowned out his words. Which was all right, because I wouldn't have understood them anyway. The medicine man heard him out, then pulled down his scarf to
reply. That's when I received my second shock of the day.

The face beneath the headdress was dusky, the nose
broad and flat, the lips thick. Against this background, the

whites of his eyes were startling. It was the kind of face you expected to see beneath the cap of a Pullman porter, or bent over your boots and grinning at its reflection in the fresh shine. The last place you would have looked for it was beside the chief of the most powerful Indian tribe in the Bitterroot. I'd known that some tribes took in Negroes out of spite for the white man, but I could think of no other instance in which one of these foundlings had risen to such influential rank. The entire party could have charged us at that moment and I would have been unable to react, I was that stunned.

For a while it seemed that there was some disagreement between the two about whether they should camp there for the night or proceed into the cleft in which the three of us were crouched. At length, however, the order was given to dismount, and as darkness crept over them, the Flatheads began setting up their lodges.

"We'll camp here for tonight," I whispered to Little Tree, after withdrawing from the opening. "Pull out before dawn, the way we came in. If they find us here we'll be wolf-meat by tomorrow night."

"Lose one day," the squaw pointed out.

"Better a day than our scalps."

"Ain't no need to pull out," said Bear.

I looked at him. Bundled up as he was aboard the litter, only his blue eyes showed, staring up at the sky.

"Suicide must look pretty good from where you sit," I said dryly.

"How many injuns we got?" he asked me.

"Four or five hundred. The whole shebang. Why?"

"You know how long it takes to shove four or five hunnert riders single file through this crack?"

"What are you getting at?"

"Them Flatheads is anxious to clear these mountains before every pass gets blocked twixt here and the plains. Many as there are, they'll save at least a day by going around the long way. Besides, Two Sisters ain't exactly the kind to favor placing his whole tribe in a situation where they could get bushwacked as easy as in here. Just sit tight. They'll be on their way by sunup tomorrow."

"And if they aren't?"

He met my gaze. "You reckon we can survive an extra day in this blizzard?"

"No."

"Then I don't see as we got much choice."

That ended the discussion. Above us, the wind squealed between broken pinnacles of ice and rock, casting bushels of dry white granules over us at ragged intervals. "How's the back?" I asked Bear.

"It ain't good," he said. "Every now and then, I get so's I can move my legs a little; sometimes I almost figure I can get up. But it don't last long."

I nodded. Then, "What do you know of a black man who rides with the Flatheads?"

The scalp-hunter stiffened. "He with them now?"

"You know him?"

"That's Black Kettle, or so he calls himself." His voice was taut. "Blackfeet talk about him all the time. According to them, he worked as a slave on a plantation down in Georgia until he got caught up in an uprising and was wounded when the overseer's men moved in with shotguns. They cut down about a dozen of them. Slaves ain't cheap, so they patched him up, give him a whipping, and told him to get back to work. Sometime later he knifed the overseer and lit a shuck for the Northwest. That's the story he give the Flatheads, anyhow. I reckon he was heading for Canada when he got took prisoner by Two Sisters."

"He dresses like a medicine man," I said.

"That's what he is. Injuns and niggers take to each other like hot corn and butter, and crazy men are powerful medicine. He had to make it sooner or later."

"Black Kettle's crazy?"

"If he was a dog, he'd of been shot a long time ago."

"I take it he doesn't care for white men."

Bear laughed, but without humor. "Next to him, Rocking Wolf is a Presbyterian minister."

"That explains it," I said.

"Explains what?"

"Why your parents were killed. I'd always wondered what prompted Two Sisters to go on the warpath that year. I'm surprised you didn't see it."

"I saw it."

"Then how come his scalp isn't in that bag?" I nodded toward the gunny sack hanging from the horn of the dun's saddle.

"Don't think I ain't tried," he said. "He's crafty. He never leaves camp, and I ain't got to the point where I'm ready to take on more than one or two hunnert Flatheads at a shot."

"Meaning that someday you will?"

"Meaning that someday I'm going to take Black Kettle's kinky scalp."

We fell silent for a moment, listening to the wind and the faint noises drifting up from the camp below us. Finally, Bear said, "Any sign of Rocking Wolf?"

"No. Maybe he's dead. I don't see how he could make it out there with neither horse nor rifle."

"We don't know for sure that he don't have a rifle. Besides, survival is an injun's business; it's the first thing he learns before he gets his feather. Likely they missed him somewhere."

"That's one feat I hope we can duplicate," I muttered.

Little Tree and I unhitched the litter and did what we could to make ourselves comfortable, which proved to be a wasted effort. The cleft acted like a bellows in reverse, sucking in cold air and cascades of snow that rattled in gusts against our heavy clothing and burned our skin like hot ashes wherever it found a chink. We didn't dare light a fire; for warmth we wrapped ourselves in our blankets and huddled together around Bear with our backs to the wind like cattle. Now and then a scent of wood smoke wafted over us from the direction of the plateau, which did nothing to improve our spirits. Further, there was no escaping the conviction that behind us, the shadows swarmed with wolves. It was going to be a long night for the three of us.

Sunup—if it could be called that, hidden as it was behind the pewter-colored overcast—found me struggling to get to my feet, working the rust out of joints I hadn't known I possessed until that morning. After relieving Little Tree of the Spencer, I crept forward to the granite promontory I had manned the previous afternoon. The plateau was a beehive of activity; Indians milled around leading horses, striking huts, extinguishing fires—in general, getting ready to depart. In the center of everything sat Two Sisters astride his painted horse, barking orders and directing the operation with sweeping gestures. While he was thus engaged, Black Kettle rode up to him. Immediately the two appeared to resume the argument they had carried out the day before, the medicine man gesticulating like a madman while his chief shook his head stubbornly. Watching, I got the impression that this was a common scene between them. Eventually Black Kettle threw up his hands, wheeled his horse, and cantered out of sight beyond the rock behind which I was crouching.

That Two Sisters had won the argument was evident. The only question that remained was what stand he had taken. Had he opted to go around the mountain the long way, or was it his intention to defy what Bear had said about him and lead the tribe straight through the cleft? If it was the latter, we were as good as dead. There was no way we were going to hitch up Bear's litter, turn around, and get out of there before the first Indian entered. I cursed myself for having taken the advice of an invalid who was more than likely suffering from delirium.

"What our plans?"

I started and swung the Spencer around, narrowly missing Little Tree's head with the side of the barrel as I did so. She had come up behind me so silently that I hadn't known she was there until she'd spoken. She was holding Ira Longbow's Dance, which I'd given her previously, in her right hand. I relaxed my hold on the rifle.

"You're doing fine," I told her. "Just keep that gun handy. If they come this way, we're going to sell our lives as dearly as possible. It worked for Custer."

Either the speech sounded better then than it does now, or Little Tree's training kept her from commenting. At any rate, it seemed to satisfy her, because she stopped asking questions I couldn't answer.

You had to hand it to the Flatheads for efficiency. Within ten minutes they had the plateau stripped of any evidence that their camp had ever existed, and were mounted and lined up along the northern edge waiting for the order to move. Beyond them, Black Kettle rode restlessly back and forth, a gray presence behind the driving sheets of snow.

For a moment Two Sisters appeared to hesitate, which was understandable. If Bear's assumption was correct, the chief had not heard from Rocking Wolf for days, and like any other uncle he was loath to depart without knowing his nephew's fate. Finally, however, he made his decision;

without a word he kneed his mount forward and led the way north—around the mountain.

We watched in silence as the column of Flatheads paraded past the opening. Last to leave was the medicine man, who spent sometime trotting about the deserted camp as if to blow off steam, casting frustrated glances in the direction of the cleft. The squaw and I flattened ourselves against the ice-covered rock wall and listened to the beating of our own hearts, louder at this point than the shrieking wind. Minutes crept by, or maybe they were just seconds; it was impossible to judge. At last Black Kettle spun the horse about and, with an angry whoop, galloped off in the others' wake.

I let out my breath and lowered the rifle, the sights of which I'd had lined up on the black man's broad chest. Beside me, Little Tree replaced the Dance's hammer with a sigh of sliding metal. For a stretch neither of us spoke.

"Hitch up the litter," I said at last. I was surprised at the steadiness of my own voice.

We took our time crossing the plateau, to avoid being spotted by stragglers as much as to ensure the scalp-hunter a comfortable ride, and reached the cover of the woods after an hour. From there we descended to the edge of a river some forty feet wide at its broadest point, where we stopped. It was one of those countless tributaries that take so many twists and turns on their way through the mountains that they wind up with either a dozen names or none at all. The wind had swept this one clean of snow, leaving the silvery surface of the ice bare but for serpentine ribbons of powder writhing across it in the wind. Its banks were lined with pine and cattails, the latter bowed beneath the weight of clinging frost and so deceptively fragile in appearance that they seemed ready to fall apart at the touch of a finger. Ice-laden hulks of fallen trees formed natural bridges across the water where they had been torn out of the ground in past storms.

"We cross?" asked Little Tree.

"I don't know," I replied. "It took a lot of punishment when the Flatheads crossed. Let me have the mare." I dismounted.

"What you do?" She got down off the chestnut and handed me the reins.

"I'll have a better idea of how much this ice can hold once I cross over." I swung into the mare's saddle. "Wait for the high sign before you start across with Bear. Lead, don't ride. If you hear it start to crack, get the hell off fast."

Out in the open, the wind was ruthless. It plucked at the brim of my hat and found its way inside my coat, billowing it out behind me. My breath froze in my nostrils and clung in crystals to the stubble on my cheeks and chin. Updrafts snatched my pants legs out of the tops of my boots, expos-bare skin to blasts of peppery snow.

Suddenly, something hard struck the ice at the mare's feet, sending up a geyser of splinters and shooting cracks out in all directions. Coming upon its heels, the sound of the shot was an anticlimax.

CHAPTER TWELVE

I left the saddle just as the mare reared, striking the ice hard on my right shoulder and rolling. The horse fled slipping and sliding in the direction from which we had come. I clawed my gun out of its holster and lay on my stomach gripping the weapon in both hands, my elbows propped up on the ice.

There was nothing to shoot at. An unbroken line of brush and pine formed a barrier along the opposite bank, behind which an army could have hidden. Even the cloud of metallic gray gunsmoke drifting across the scene had been snatched away by the wind so fast that it was impossible to tell where it had originated. In a game of snipers, I was the only visible target for miles.

"Get up, white skin!"

Nearly drowned out as it was by the wailing gale, there was still no mistaking that voice. I remained prone.

Another bullet spanged off the ice near my left elbow, spitting bits of crystal into my face. The shot echoed growlingly into the distance. I got up.

"I would have bet money you'd lost your rifle back at Devil's Crack," I told Rocking Wolf. I held the gun against my right hip.

"You would have lost."

I tried to place where the voice was coming from, but the wind roaring in my ears made that impossible.

"You did well, white skin," it continued. "I have the use

of only one leg. When last we spoke the pain was too great for me to take aim. Since then I have grown used to it. Had I not, I would never have been able to come this far, where I knew you would one day pass." He snapped off another shot, which whizzed past my ear and struck the ice ten feet behind me. Hairline cracks leaped out across the surface.

"Where is Mountain That Walks?"

I hesitated a beat before answering. It had just dawned on me that from where Rocking Wolf was—wherever he was—Bear and his squaw were invisible. "He's dead," I said.

"You lie." A fourth bullet pierced the ice directly in front of me. Water splattered over my boots. I leaped backward.

"It's the truth." I spread my legs to distribute my weight; the surface was growing spongy. "He had a bullet in his back, put there by the bounty hunters we met west of the Crack. The bullet finally moved. I buried him twenty miles back."

There was no reply. I began to feel cold where my body had come into contact with the clammy surface of the ice. Finally the voice called out again.

"Surrender your gun, white skin. Slide it across the ice. The one in your belt as well."

I obeyed. The revolver skidded ten feet and came to a stop just past the halfway point. The Colt followed, sliding beyond that and losing itself in the cattails on the other side. At that moment Rocking Wolf stepped out from behind a tangle of brambles and began hobbling toward me.

Purple bruises had swollen his face into a caricature; his left eye was a crescent glittering between folds of puffy flesh and his lips were thick and torn. His bearskin hung in tatters from his thickset frame. He held the Winchester cradled in his left arm, the right supporting his weight upon a forked limb thrust beneath the armpit. The leg on that side shattered, most likely, in his fall—dragged uselessly behind him. Any pretense he had made previously of masking his emotions had been abandoned, for the face that confronted me was twisted with hatred beyond even its physical mutilation.

He stopped with his feet planted on either side of the abandoned Deane-Adams and raised the rifle to the level of my chest. "Do not turn away," he barked. His swollen lips got in the way of his consonants, slurring them. "You should be prepared to face your handiwork."

"I don't suppose it would do any good to deny I had anything to do with it," I said.

"Do not waste my time. I am through listening." He shifted the makeshift crutch a little so that he could steady the rifle with his other hand. Not that he really had to, at that range, but he wanted to prolong the moment.

I decided that if Little Tree were going to make a move from the cover of the brush behind me, she would have done so by now. Stooping suddenly, I scooped the bowie knife out of my right boot and followed through in an underhand fling, sending the blade whistling in the general direction of the Indian's squat torso.

It didn't land point first, of course; that was too much to hope for under the circumstances. What mattered was that Rocking Wolf thought it would. He moved to dodge it even as the leather-bound handle swung around and bounced harmlessly off his chest; in so doing, he threw too much weight onto the crutch and it slipped out from under him. By that time I was in motion, charging head down like a maddened bull. He fired. Something hot seared my right cheek, too late. I struck him head first in the midsection, and we went down together. The rifle spun from his grip and clattered away out of reach.

A town-bred white man is no match for a wild Indian at the best of times, but I'd counted on Rocking Wolf's injury giving me an edge. What I hadn't counted on was my own injury. Mountain air goes no further toward healing a fractured skull than that at sea level, and in any case it isn't advisable to use the damaged instrument as a weapon. My vision blurred, doubled. I saw two Deane-Adams revolvers lying side by side on the ice and grabbed for the wrong one, coming up with a handful of empty air. By that time the Indian had found his wind; cocking his good leg, he planted his foot against my chest and pushed hard. I reeled backward and was forced to execute a fancy roll to avoid splitting my head open all over again when I struck the ice.

The Indian reached out blindly and closed his fingers over the bowie knife. Rolling over onto his stomach, he pulled himself toward me frantically, dragging his useless right leg behind him, one hand clutching the knife like an ice pick. When he was close enough, he raised the weapon high over his head and stabbed downward. I rolled again, just as the blade shattered the ice where my head had been, and before he could react, I straddled his back, locking my arms around his throat from behind.

It was no good; though my vision had corrected itself, my head was pounding and I was weak as a baby. He stabbed back and up with the knife, forcing me to break my grip to keep the blade from slashing open my ribcage. At the same time he hooked my ankle with his good left leg and arched his back, flipping me off. The impact of my fall blinded me for an instant. The first thing I saw when my senses returned was Rocking Wolf on his knees before me, the hand holding the knife poised over his head in striking position.

He had started the downward swing when a shot rang out and his forehead exploded. Blood and bits of bone spattered my face. The knife dropped from his hand and clattered to the ice. Slowly, as if he had changed his mind, he sank back onto his heels and just as slowly toppled over sideways. His body jerked spasmodically for a moment, then lay still.

I didn't waste any time after that. When you hear a shot you weren't expecting, the first rule is that you look around for a weapon. I wasn't about to throw away my cards without knowing for sure whether it was Little Tree who had fired. I flopped over onto my stomach and began crawling toward my gun.

I was within reach of it when there was another explosion and the revolver spun away from me, arcing across the now-wet surface of the ice. Immediately I rolled in the opposite direction and came to rest on my stomach behind Rocking Wolf's still form. Once there I risked a quick glance toward the bank where I had left my companions, for it was there that the shots had originated.

Church was standing on the edge of the ice holding Bear's Spencer in both hands. His undersize frame was impossible to mistake even in that driving snow. The butt of what I took to be Ira Longbow's Dance protruded above his holster. Behind him, Homer Strakey's equally recognizable bulk stood in a position where he could keep an eye on both Bear and Little Tree. His stance told me he was armed. Although I couldn't see it, I knew he had his dead son's old-fashioned percussion cap pistol in one hand. What with the blizzard and the drama that had been taking place on the ice, it had been no feat for the two to sneak up on my companions and relieve them of their weapons. Now I knew why Little Tree hadn't fired at the Indian when it seemed she'd had the chance.

"Looks like you owe me again, Murdock!" cried Church. His scarf was tied loosely around his scrawny neck, the ends flapping in the wind. "I can't abide watching no injun kill no white man."

"So you'll do it instead," I finished.

"Got to. You got so's I can't go around you no more, and I'm tired of dogging you. Now, get up from behind that dead injun."

"I'd rather not."

His sloping shoulders heaved in a mighty sigh. "We got to go through this all over again? Homer!"

On cue, Strakey stepped forward and snatched out his right arm, placing the muzzle of the pistol against the squaw's right temple. She stood still as the tree for which she was named.

"Why don't you just move on?" I demanded, stalling for time. "You've got Anderson."

"I do for a fact—all wrapped up like Christmas morning. How'd he get that way?"

I told him.

"Well, well." He sounded pleased. "So one of us did hit him, after all. The offer's tempting, Murdock, but it ain't enough."

"Why not?"

"There's a good day's ride between here and Staghorn; I think me and the old man would enjoy it more if we didn't have to spend all our time looking over our shoulders. I'll take my chances on the squaw, but you're another brand of bacon. Now, are you going to get up from behind that stiff or am I going to have to ask Homer to put a ball through the squaw's head? He's been itching to use that thing ever since you turned him into a candle back at Anderson's cabin."

"What makes you think that'll work with me?" I asked. "Maybe I don't care what happens to her."

"All right, Homer, blow her brains out."

"Hold it! I'll get up."

Still I hesitated, but not just because I didn't want to get killed, which of course I didn't. In stepping forward to put the pistol against Little Tree's head, Strakey had turned his back on Bear's litter. That was evidently the opportunity for which the scalp-hunter had been waiting. Awkwardly and with great effort—he was, after all, shaking off the paralysis of days—he swung his legs out from under the covers and rose like a gigantic specter behind the old man's tensed form.

"Come on!" To show he meant business, Church slapped a bullet from the Spencer into Rocking Wolf's body. The corpse jerked like a kicked sandbag. Another cartridge was racked into place. I climbed to my feet.

"Step clear of the stiff," ordered the bounty hunter.

I took my time obeying. He grew impatient.

"Homer!"

But Homer wasn't listening. At that moment, the scalp-hunter threw his massive arms around the big old man and squeezed, lifting him up in the air as he did so to throw the pistol off target. The ball was released with a snap, missing Little Tree by a least a foot. Simultaneously I heard the crackling noise of ribs giving away beneath the pressure. Strakey screamed through his teeth, a high, chuckling wail that put me in mind of his dead son's nervous giggle.

Church's reaction was not immediate; he had called to his partner and had heard the expected shot. But at the sound of the scream he took a step backward and turned his head. It was just what I needed.

He realized his mistake almost in the next instant, but by then it was too late. I had already dived and come up on my knees with the Deane-Adams gripped in both hands, and when he snapped his head back in my direction I pumped all five bullets into his chest.

For a space I regretted that it wasn't a six-shooter, as the bounty hunter hovered there seemingly unaffected by his wounds, the rifle firmly in his grip. But then his knees buckled and he folded to the ground. The Spencer flopped free.

Homer Strakey's spine snapped with a report like a pistol shot. Bear, who had lifted the old man's body high over his head to deliver the final blow, flung it, rag-doll fashion, to the earth. Clad in skins as he was, his features blurred by the swirling snow, the mountaineer might have been one of those legendary manlike beasts the Indians of the North call the Sasquatch. Then his knees began to shake and the image was dispelled.

I made my way over to the bank, but not before reloading my revolver from the dwindling supply of cartridges on my belt, on the off chance that one of the bounty hunters might still be alive. I needn't have bothered; neither of them was about to get up this side of Judgment Day. I picked up the Spencer and freed Church's body of his gun belt and the Dance he had taken from Little Tree. Strakey's cap-and-ball I left to the elements like the useless toy it was once its load had been fired.

"Anybody hurt?" I inquired.

Little Tree shook her head. She had gone to her mate's side and had an arm around him; he cast it off and stood there swaying. "Let's ride," he said. "Likely them Flatheads heard all that shooting and are on their way here already."

"When did the bullet shift?" I asked him.

"Just before we stopped." He had turned and, walking on unsteady legs, crossed over to his horse to unhitch the litter. "I didn't say nothing at the time because I wasn't sure. It was just a tingle. What difference does it make? It shifted. Find that nag of yours and let's ride."

"Ease up. If that bullet's as mobile as that, you're running a risk every time you take a step."

"Save that stuff for when you hang out your shingle," he retorted, tossing the litter aside with a powerful thrust of the left arm. He winced and placed what he thought was a surreptitious hand against his injury. I pretended not to notice.

The mare hadn't wandered far. I found it munching at a blackberry bush on the edge of the forest and led it back to the riverbank, where it became so troublesome at the scent of gunpowder and death that I had to tether it to the trunk of a storm-shattered pine while I sought out the bounty hunters' horses. These were hobbled a hundred yards upstream behind a steep snowbank. I chose one—a black with a yellow blaze and stockings to match—for Little Tree, and after removing the other's saddle and bridle, cut it loose and shooed it away. There was no sense in making things easy for Lop Ear and company. Only as I stood watching it canter away toward the comparative openness of the forest did I realize that I had just released a mount far better than the one I was riding. Well, I had gotten used to the aging chestnut anyway. I threw the extra saddle and bridle into the snowbank and rejoined Bear and Little Tree with the black.

Crossing was tricky. I went first, leading the mare, and when I had reached the opposite bank, Little Tree struck out with her new mount, followed by Bear leading the big dun. When he was halfway across, the ice hammocked, squirting water up through its cracks and groaning ominously. He stopped, but as the noise continued it became apparent that standing still was no safer than moving and he resumed with caution. There were two inches of water on top of the ice by the time he and the horse stepped up onto dry land, but the surface remained intact. From a distance it might have been two feet thick.

"We'll stop here," Bear said.

"We've eight hours of daylight left," I pointed out. "What about the Indians?"

"This is where we make our stand."

"Nice last words. Too bad there won't be anybody left to carve them on your tombstone." I spoke bitterly.

"We ain't about to outrun them, that's for sure. And a river's good a place as any to face off. Better than most." He held out his hand for the Spencer. I gave it to him reluctantly.

"Tether the horses clear of the firing line," he told Little Tree, handing her his reins. When she moved off, leading all three animals, he inclined his head toward the gun in my holster. "You're going to have to use a little more economy when it comes to shooting Flatheads. You used four too many on Church."

"Do I tell you how to scalp Indians?" I snapped.

"Just a suggestion."

The Indians came at noon. By that time, entrenched amid the cattails between Bear and the squaw—who was armed once again with the Dance—my gun in hand and the rest of the captured iron within reach, I had given up on them entirely. I was about to say so when the sound of galloping hoofs reached me faintly over the incessant whine of the wind. A soft rumble at first, in seconds it swelled to a roar. The scalp-hunter settled his Spencer into a groove he had hollowed out previously atop an old muskrat den and sighted in on the spot across the river where we had left the bodies for bait.

"Don't nobody fire until I give the word," he said.

They came streaming out of the forest on the other side, a loose wedge of warriors with Two Sisters and Black Kettle mounted at the point. From there the momentum slowed until, drawing near the corpses, they halted. A brave sprang down from his horse and stooped to examine each of the bodies. Rising, he cast a glance across the river, spotted Rocking Wolf sprawled face down in the middle, and pointed.

The chief had already noticed. He nodded reflectively, after which he and the medicine man fell into animated conversation. At one point the latter paused to gaze along the opposite bank, then suddenly raised his right arm and thrust a finger straight at us. I buried my face in my arms. When no bullets followed the gesture, however, I returned my attention to the Indians. It appeared that Two Sisters and Black Kettle were arguing once again, this time over whether they should charge across and begin pursuit immediately or follow the bank and cross farther upstream to avoid a possible ambush, with the medicine man in favor of the former. This time he won. Under instructions from the chief, punctuated once again by numerous gestures, the Flatheads lined up along the riverbank in what my old cavalry sergeant would call charge formation.

"Remember," Bear muttered, "not until I give the word."

They started across in a tight line, unslinging their bows and rifles as they went. The ice bowed dangerously beneath their collective weight. I stretched out full length on my stomach and held the Deane-Adams with my arms resting on a knot of tangled cattails, awaiting the order to fire. It didn't come when I expected it, with the result that I almost gave the game away with a premature shot. Even then Bear remained silent. Out of the corner of my eye I caught a glimpse of his bearded profile; his teeth were showing and the skin over his brow was taut. By that time the Indians were so close I imagined I could smell the mingled stenches of horse and rancid bear grease.

"Fire!" His voice was shrill.

Our first shots crackled like burning wood. Two braves fell, shrieking as they spun from their horses. The third bullet—I think it came from the Spencer—struck Black Kettle's horse and it crashed over onto its side, spilling the medicine man off its back and smashing through the ice where it fell. That sparked off a chain reaction, and as we continued firing the river became a confused tangle of tumbling warriors and horses screaming and thrashing in the black water. Bodies, both of horses and men, were so thick that there was no longer any need to take aim; we just kept pumping lead into the fray like hunters heading off a herd of stampeding buffalo. In seconds the holes in the ice were rounded up with bobbing corpses.

I had emptied both the five-shot and Church's Navy Colt and was reaching for Rocking Wolf's Winchester when Two Sisters gave the order to retreat. Ducking lead, the braves gathered up what dead they could get their hands on and thrashed their way back toward the opposite bank, twisting around now and then to snap off a shot in our direction. Bear and I kept hammering away at their backs until they vanished among the trees.

"They'll try again," said the scalp-hunter. "Next time they'll be more savvy."

He took in his breath suddenly, and I paused in my reloading to look at him. He was staring in the direction of the river. I followed his gaze. Something was bobbing in the water.

At first I thought it was a corpse the Indians had overlooked, but as I watched I saw that it wasn't a corpse at all, but a live warrior swimming frantically toward the broken edge of the ice. I squinted through the flying snow; it was Black Kettle. Unseated from his horse, he had plunged into the river and was straining every muscle to reach the safety of the ice before he was either dragged down by the weight of his furs or picked off by our guns. Tight, glistening wet curls spilled over his shoulders and down his back, his buffalo horn headgear having been discarded.

"Let me have the knife." Bear's tone was strained. When I hesitated, he reached back and snatched the bowie out of my boot. In another moment he was on his feet and striding out over what was left of the ice.

"Bear!" I shouted. It was no good. He had eyes and ears only for the man in the water.

He reached the jagged edge just as Black Kettle lunged forward and grabbed hold of it with both hands. The medicine man's gasp of relief was choked off as he saw the fur boots planted in front of him and looked up at Anderson's towering figure. I saw the whites of his eyes bulge in horror, and then Bear bent down, snatched a handful of his kinky hair, and with the other hand swept the blade of the bowie from left to right across Black Kettle's throat. Arterial blood spurted out three feet in a bright red stream; his gurgling cry was torn to shreds by the wind. The water turned pink around him. Now only Bear's grip on his hair kept the medicine man from sliding beneath the surface, and in another moment, as the scalp-hunter gathered a bigger fistful and made use of the knife once again, the river snatched away the final traces and swept them—body, blood and all—downstream.

I had seen too much in one day. When Bear straightened, holding aloft his bloody trophy for all to see, I turned my head and was sick.

CHAPTER THIRTEEN

Lying beside me, Little Tree was strangely silent. I overcame my nausea long enough to ask if she was all right. She wasn't.

"Bear!"

I had to call a second time before he heard me. Finally he turned and, still holding the dripping scalp, made his way shakily across the ice; the sluggishness in his right leg told me that some of the paralysis was still with him. "What is it?" he demanded, his chest heaving.

"Your squaw's dead."

I had been in no mood to break it to him gently. Now I regretted my bluntness. He dropped the scalp and fell to his knees at Little Tree's side, gathered her in his arms and tried to get her to raise herself. It was no use; the blood was already beginning to congeal where a bullet from a Flathead rifle had made jelly out of the back of her head on its way out of her brain.

"I hope the scalp was worth it," I said.

I regretted that too, but for a more personal reason, as without warning he let go of the corpse and swept his knife around in a broad arc with the intent of decapitating me. I ducked just as the blade swished past, knocking off my hat. Before he could come back the other way I fisted my revolver and, taking advantage of his hunched-over position, threw all my weight into a punch straight at his bearded jaw. I felt the jar all the way to my shoulder as I connected. That was more than I could say for Bear, who shook his head as if to rid himself of a moth trapped in his whiskers, gathered the front of my collar in one tremendous fist, and without so much as a grunt of exertion lifted me off my feet and held me dangling twenty-four inches above the ground. His eyes were bloodshot, his face purple.

"Now," he said, balancing the knife in his other hand, "let's see what you et for breakfast."

"You'll have to take my word for it." I stretched out my right arm, which was only now beginning to ache, and planted the muzzle of the Deane-Adams between his bushy brows. "This time there's no broken firing pin."

I could tell it wasn't working. He was going to use the knife, and it didn't matter whether I pulled the trigger or not, because with his last reflex he was going to let open my belly. We were both dead. All that remained was the burying. Judge Blackthorne was going to be confused as hell when he learned what had happened to me. I began to squeeze the trigger.

The cylinder was already turning when the scalp-hunter's face twisted into a mask of pain and he lost his grip on the knife. It hit the snow only an instant before he did. I pulled loose from his weakened hold on my collar, landed on my feet, and prepared to finish the job I had started, for the gun was still in my hand.

He was stretched before me, unable to move. All my experience told me to fire and get it over with. Even if he wasn't bluffing, and the bullet in his back had in fact shifted, we would both be better off if I put him out his misery and rode on. There was no doubt in my mind that that was the only thing to do, so of course I didn't do it. I let the hammer down gently and put the gun away.

"How bad is it this time?" I asked him.

"Don't know." His feet shifted slightly in the snow. "I'm starting to feel something. A tingle."

"You're lucky. It probably moved again when you hit the ground. It could just as easily have cut a cord and killed you. Can you ride?"

"Go to hell."

"I'm sorry about Little Tree," I said. "But's she's dead and those Indians are due back any time. If you can't ride, I'll have to rig another litter. From now on we keep moving until we get to town."

"Do what you want. I'm staying."

"Like hell you are. Little Tree and I didn't bring you this far just to let you commit suicide. She's dead because of you. Are you saying that doesn't mean anything?"

He didn't reply. I gaped at him.

"That's what you're saying, isn't it?" I arranged my face into a sneer. "You're pathetic. It wasn't enough that you threw away your life on vengeance; you had to toss hers out too. Now that it's come down to a choice, you've chosen to go out in a blaze of glory. Glory, hell! You're giving up."

Roaring in rage, he threw himself over onto his stomach and wriggled through the snow toward where he had left his Spencer. He had his hand on it when I took two steps and pinned it, hand and all, beneath my boot.

"'Mountain That Walks!'" I taunted, sneering down at him. "You can't even crawl."

He let his face fall forward into the snow.

I reached down, snatched the rifle out of his grip, and jacked out all the shells. "Better pick them up," I advised, tossing the weapon down beside him. "You haven't got that many to spare."

He was still lying there when I mounted the mare and rode off. I can't say now whether I intended to leave him to his fate or if I thought my leaving might shake him out of it and get him to follow me. I was sure he could ride. How I really felt is a moot point, though, because I hadn't made half a mile through the steep drifts that blanketed the foothills when I spotted the blue uniforms riding toward me from the direction of Staghorn. I reined in and threw a leg over the horn of my saddle to wait.

They seemed to be taking an inordinately long time about approaching until I realized that they were doing so by design. They had heard shooting and had come running. As far as they were concerned, I was the enemy. My suspicions were confirmed when, drawing within rifle range, they spread out, dismounted, and knelt in the snow beside their horses with their rifles braced in firing position. There were fifteen of them, wearing army blue oilskin slickers over their woolen winter uniforms.

"You, there!" This from a rail-thin horse soldier near the center of the line, a sunburned youthful type with a hollow, drillmaster's voice, matter-of-fact and without inflection. "Throw down your weapons and dismount!"

I didn't argue. I unholstered the Deane-Adams for the ten thousandth time and flung it away out of temptation's reach. Next came Church's Colt, and then the rifle I had captured from Rocking Wolf. I got out of the saddle as slowly as I could without losing my balance and falling, which would undoubtedly have provoked the order to fire; he had that kind of voice.

"Now the hat. Remove it with two fingers and scale it away."

He was no fool. I did as directed. None of the men left his ready crouch even then.

"Identify yourself."

"Page Murdock, deputy U.S. marshal, Helena." I was careful to keep my hands within sight. "I have a badge, if you'd care to see it."

Apparently he didn't. He gave the order to mount, and after much floundering and soldierly cursing I was surrounded by men on horseback.

"Sergeant, his weapons." Up close, the officer wasn't quite the young man I'd thought him to be; he had a blond moustache and creases beneath his vague gray eyes. His face was gaunt beneath the brim of his campaign hat, his complexion nearly as dark as an Indian's. Little lumps of determination stood out on either side of his jaw.

The sergeant, whose square, black-moustached features looked as if they had come up against more than one bony fist in their time—once quite recently—dismounted and fished the revolvers and rifle out of the snow where I'd thrown them, then handed them up to his superior, who examined them in an offhanded fashion.

"Captain Amos Trainer, Fort Benton," he said in his clipped monotone. He made Two Sisters sound emotional by comparison.

"You're a long way from home, Captain."

He ignored that, pretending to be interested in the engraving on the side of the rifle. "We were told by the sheriff in Staghorn to look out for a mean-looking bastard riding a no-good chestnut mare. His description, not mine."

"You didn't seem to have any trouble identifying me by it," I said. "How is Henry?" I bent to retrieve my hat.

"He's dead."

I paused in mid-stoop, then snatched hold of the hat and shook it free of snow, as if that were the most important job in the world. I put it on and carefully creased the brim. "Who?"

"Nobody you'd know. About a week ago, a punk shell from Wyoming got drunk and called him out."

"Faster?"

He shook his head. "Fast as. They fired at the same time. The punk was dead when he hit the floor. Goodnight died the next morning. He never regained consciousness."

"Two years ago the punk would never have cleared leather. Who's the new sheriff?"

"You're looking at him. When there was no word from the man we sent here, General Clifton sent out this patrol to hunt down and arrest Bear Anderson, the Indian murderer. Goodnight was shot the evening we arrived. I wired the general, who wired the governor, who placed me in charge until the local citizenry can hold an election."

"Bet that pleased the general."

Something bordering on a smile passed across the officer's gaunt features. He swung open the rifle's lever, found the chamber empty, frowned, replaced it. "I was told you'd gone into the mountains after an escaped prisoner. Where is he?"

"You don't want to stand out here in this blizzard while I tell you that one," I assured him.

"We heard some shooting a while ago. You can start with that."

"I had a run-in with Two Sisters about a half-mile back."

"Alone? How many guns can you fire at one time, Deputy?"

I sighed. "I'm tired of arguing, Captain. Bear Anderson's back there, and he needs medical help."

He glared at me. "I think you'd better start explaining."

I took a deep breath and told him what I could, including the fate of the bounty hunters his commanding officer had hired. He listened in silence.

"Mount up, Sergeant," he said when I had finished.

The sergeant had been standing behind me. Now he stepped into leather, oilskin rustling, and accepted the revolvers and rifles from his superior.

"I'm going along," I said.

"That's what you think. Sergeant!"

"Yes, sir." The sergeant saluted. He spoke with a Georgia drawl; I found myself wondering what rank he had held in the Confederate Army, and if we might have met somewhere before, across a smoke-enshrouded battlefield. He was too old not to have served.

"Detail two men to stay here and keep an eye on Mr. Murdock. Orders are to shoot to kill if he tries anything." He gathered up his reins and reached back to flick open the flap securing his side arm in its holster. It was an Army Colt; what else was there, here in Colt country?

"I'm going along for your protection," I explained. "If you go in there half-cocked, you're going to lose most of your men."

He smiled twistedly. "Against one man, Deputy? One *wounded* man?"

I said, "The Flatheads number over five hundred, and they haven't been able to take him in fifteen years. And wounded or not, he just killed two men, one of them with his bare hands. If he sees me with you—armed—he might go with you peacefully."

"You're not sure?"

"He tried to kill me a little while ago."

"You don't inspire confidence, Deputy."

"That's your job, Captain. I'm just a public servant."

"Very well. Sergeant!" He nodded at the non-com, who handed me my weapons. I accepted them and returned each to its proper holder.

"But, remember," added the officer, "my orders stand to shoot to kill in the event you cross us."

"I expected no less from the U. S. Army," I replied, and mounted the mare.

Heading back toward the river, I asked Captain Trainer what he was doing out there.

"We were on our way back from our first patrol when

we heard the shots," he said.

"Isn't that neglecting your responsibilities as sheriff?" I asked.

"Not at all. There's no reason I can't fulfill my duties to the U.S. government as well as to the voters."

"Funny, I thought they were one and the same."

"Column of twos, Sergeant," he said, ignoring my comment.

We came upon him just as he was preparing to straddle the dun. Little Tree's body was nowhere to be seen; a mound of snow, marked at one end by a pine bough standing upright, explained his delay in leaving. He saw us approaching, but made no move toward the Spencer in his saddle scabbard. He mounted carefully and sat watching us.

"You said he was wounded," snapped Trainer, drawing his Colt. He signaled halt.

"I said wounded. Not dead."

"Look at the size of him." This from the sergeant. "I wish I'd brought my buffalo gun."

"Just keep him covered." Trainer raised his voice. "Bear Anderson! This is the U. S. Army! Throw down your weapons and surrender!"

The wind whistled.

"Prepare to dismount, Sergeant."

"Prepare to dismount!" bawled the sergeant. Leather creaked.

"You with them, Page?" The scalp-hunter spoke quietly.

I said I was. He nodded. "Just as well. I was getting too slow anyway." He slid the Spencer from its scabbard—the captain cocked the hammer of his Colt—and, swinging the rifle by its barrel, hurled it out into the middle of the river. It struck with a crash, bobbed once, and slid beneath the surface.

The unexpected action distracted us. While we were watching it, Bear unsheathed his bowie knife and plunged it into his breast.

CHAPTER FOURTEEN

I had started forward before he hit the ground. Trainer grabbed my arm.

"Stay back! It might be a trick."

I pulled my arm free and kicked the mare forward. Bear was lying in a hunched position at his horse's feet, breathing heavily. The big dun, anxious, shifted its weight from one front hoof to the other and snorted steam. I dismounted and turned the scalp-hunter over onto his back. The bowie was jammed up to its hilt just below the curve of his chest; blood was spreading slowly.

"Who's got a clean kerchief?" I demanded of the troopers who has come forward to look down at the legend of the Bitterroot.

"Ain't nobody got a clean kerchief after three days on patrol," the sergeant said, dismounting. "But here." He untied the yellow cloth from around his neck and handed it to me.

Pulling the knife from Bear's breast was only a little easier than loosening an axe sunk in a maple stump, but by grabbing hold of the hilt and bracing my other hand against his shoulder I succeeded in drawing it out. Then the bleeding began in earnest. I tore open his bearskin and shirt and poked the end of the kerchief into the wound. He shuddered.

"Some scalp-hunter you are," I told him. "You can't even kill yourself. That bearskin saved your life."

"I always did hate it," he said, grunting through his teeth.

I undid my belt, pulled it free, and strapped it around his chest inside his shirt to secure the makeshift bandage. It barely reached. I had to use the bloody knife to make a new hole in the leather before I could fasten it.

"How long do you think that will hold?" Trainer asked.

"Long enough to get him into Staghorn, I hope," I said. "If he lives that long."

"He won't."

"Ordinarily, I'd agree with you. But people like Bear Anderson don't just die."

"I can't understand it. If he wanted to commit suicide, why didn't he just let us shoot him?"

"I like to do some things for myself," Bear grunted. Then he lost consciousness.

"Will you look at that!" the sergeant exclaimed suddenly.

I looked up. He was pointing across the river.

A pack of wolves thronged the opposite bank, snarling and slashing at one another over the bounty hunters' now-frozen bodies. On the outer edge of the pack, Lop Ear himself, head down and teeth bared, eyed the soldiers warily. His hackles bristled. The sergeant hooked his rifle out of its scabbard, nestled the butt against his shoulder, and fired.

The pack scattered, all except Lop Ear, who stood his ground. The sergeant fired again. This time the big leader howled and tried to rear, but the bullet had smashed a hind leg. The rifle crashed a third time. The wolf fell over onto its right shoulder, kicked, and lay still. Steam rose from its body.

"Wolves," spat the sergeant, lowering the rifle. "I hate 'em."

Expecting Bear to ride with a bullet in his back and a

knife wound in his chest was out of the question, so the soldiers and I set about constructing a new litter while the captain paced the riverbank, twisting a gloved fist in a gloved palm and firing anxious glances from time to time across the water, where the Indians remained an unseen presence. On that side, gangs of wolves heaved and tore at the carcasses of the bounty hunters and their dead leader, bolting great bloody chunks of meat and hair in their eagerness to fill their bellies before they were shouldered aside by the others. Pleading low ammunition, Trainer had put a stop to any more shooting of the animals, and so we were forced to work to the accompaniment of their greedy slurps and snarls. At last we had the scalp-hunter secured to the rig and hitched once again behind the dun; with me in charge of it and troopers leading my mare and the black behind their mounts, we pulled out.

The blizzard had begun to wind down by the time we reached the foothills. That night the cloud cover broke, allowing a ragged splinter of moon to glimmer down and set aglow the rolling whiteness that surrounded us. We made no camp, having fed and watered our horses at the river. As it turned out, though, we needn't have been concerned about pursuit, as by sunrise—a brilliant, sparkling sunrise, the first such in many days—we had yet to be overtaken. Already it seemed that Black Kettle's loss had begun to change the character of the Flathead nation. We stopped for a short rest at noon, and by the close of the second day we were on the outskirts of Staghorn, where the smell of wood smoke quickened the pace of even the most exhausted of our mounts.

The main street was deserted, which came as no surprise since it was piled with snow up to the tops of the hitching rails on either side. We came to a halt in front of the darkened barbershop.

"Sergeant, see if you can wake Staghorn's excuse for a doctor," ordered Captain Trainer.

"Not him," I said.

"Open your eyes, Deputy. Right now, Ezra Wilson is the only thing available. Every road to town is blocked."

"I'd rather do the job myself."

The sergeant banged on the door with the butt of his revolver and kept banging until a light came on inside the shop. The door flew inward and Ezra Wilson, in nightshirt and cap, started out onto the threshold.

"What the hell—oh, good evening, Captain." He had spotted the mounted troopers.

"We've a wounded man here, Wilson," said the captain. "How are you at surgery?"

"At this hour?"

"At any hour. Never mind. Get moving, Sergeant. I want two strong men on each end of that litter. Get him inside."

It was the work of two minutes for the delegated men to unhitch the litter, hoist it, and staggering beneath their burden, shuttle it past Wilson into the shop. The troopers transferred the patient from the litter to the bed in the back room.

"Who in perdition is *that*?" Wilson stared pop-eyed at the giant that was revealed when the blankets covering him were peeled back. Bear was conscious and breathing with great effort.

"That there's the man who might just make you famous if you pull him through, Doc," volunteered the sergeant. "That there's Bear Anderson."

The eyes started farther. "Anderson? The scalp-hunter?"

"Is there any other?" I retorted. "Look, he's got a bullet in his back, and I think it's leaning up against his spine. Can you take it out?"

"I don't know. I never tried anything like that. And I'm not about to try now. I don't treat murderers."

"You'll treat this one." I drew my gun.

Wilson stared at it for a moment. Then he smiled. "You wouldn't shoot."

I shattered the glass chimney of the lamp he was holding with one shot. He lost his grip on the base and had to stoop to catch it before it hit the floor. The flame flickered violently.

"Are you crazy?" Trainer exclaimed. "You could have burned us up!"

I removed the empty shell from the cylinder and replaced it with a fresh cartridge. "I have faith in Wilson. He's good with his hands. That's why he's a barber." I spun the cylinder. "What about it, Ezra? Are you going to operate?"

He was standing there holding the still-burning lamp in both hands. He opened his mouth, closed it. "I'll wash up." He set down the lamp and stepped out through the side door.

"You're something new in lawmen," said the captain, studying me curiously.

I holstered the gun, looked around, found another lamp, and transferred its chimney to the one the barber had just relinquished. "You and my boss would get along famously," I told him. "He says the same thing."

Ezra Wilson returned a few minutes later wearing the same clothes he'd had on when I left his shop the last time. "Turn him over," he mumbled, opening his medical bag and setting out the contents on the table beside the bed.

"See to his chest first," I said. "He's been stabbed."

"Anything else?" His tone was ironic.

"What would you like?"

"Room. I need room to work."

Captain Trainer dismissed everyone except the sergeant. Then the non-com and I helped Wilson strip off Bear's shirt and bearskin. His chest was a battlefield of scars old and new, but the barber was interested in only one. He undid the belt I had fastened around the huge torso and slowly drew out the kerchief.

"Christ," he said, looking at the bloody relic. "Why didn't you stuff your hat in while you were at it?"

He opened a bottle of alcohol and poured it into the wound. The scalp-hunter arched his back, sucking air in through his teeth.

"Laudanum!" Wilson barked. "Cabinet, top shelf. Hurry!"

The captain reached down the square bottle and handed it to him. He pulled out the stopper with his teeth, measured a portion of its contents into a shot glass on the table, put it to Bear's lips. The big man gulped it down greedily, his head supported by the barber's other hand. Almost immediately he relaxed and his breathing returned to normal. Wilson looked at me sideways.

"It does have its uses, you see," he said.

He finished cleaning the wound and applied a patch, securing it with sticking-plaster, then nodded to us. The sergeant and I helped him turn the patient over onto his chest. "Turn up the lamp," said Wilson. I obeyed. A warm yellow glow spread over the bed. Fresh shadows crawled up the wall on the other side.

"It's healed over," the barber observed. "I'll have to reopen." He reached for the laudanum bottle and glass. I took hold of his arm.

"He's had enough," I said.

He looked at me. "It's not for him."

I hesitated. He held his hands up in front of my face. They were shaking. I released my grip.

I watched the expressions on the two soldiers' faces as the barber poured himself a measure of the narcotic— nearly twice what he'd given Bear—and tossed it down as if it were a shot of watered-down whiskey. To say that they were thunderstruck would be an understatement. But they kept their mouths shut.

There was a clock somewhere in the building; the ticks reverberated like explosions in that overheated room as Wilson cut with his scalpel and probed inside the wound with alcohol-soaked fingers. At length he straightened and wiped the blood off on a towel.

"It's deep," he said. "Maybe too deep. I'm just a barber. I don't know anything about backs."

"Can you get it out?" I asked.

"No question about that. The question is, what'll happen when I do it? It's fifty-fifty I might kill or cripple him." He looked at the captain. "Will you take the responsibility?"

That was a tough one. I could see Trainer weighing the odds. It was a decision that could affect his career, and not for the better. Finally he nodded. "Go ahead," he said. "Whatever happens, I'll back you up."

Under Wilson's direction, I poured more alcohol over his hands while he held them over a basin on the table. He shook them dry. Then he seized a pair of metal tongs and had me repeat the procedure with them.

"Hold up the lamp," he told me. As I did so, allowing the light to flood into the gaping hole, he spread the flesh around it with his fingers. A drop of sweat rolled down his nose. He wiped it off on his rolled-up sleeve.

"There it is," he said. "See it?"

I leaned over for a closer look. Framed between his fingers, a dark and shadowy something showed deep in the wound. "So that's what they look like after they hit," I said.

"Of course. What did you expect?"

"I don't know. I put them in. I don't take them out."

"You've got the easy job."

He inserted the tongs. As he worked, a fresh bud of perspiration started out on the bridge of his nose and began the long crawl downward. I removed my kerchief—this time clean didn't matter—and mopped his face gently. His breath came sibilantly through his nostrils. After what seemed an eternity he drew out the tongs, straightened, and with an exhausted sweep of his right arm hurled the offending substance clanging into the basin.

"What's the verdict?" I asked him.

He picked up the discarded scalpel from the basin and extended it to me. "Care to do the honors?"

I stared at him uncomprehendingly. Finally he shrugged and used the pointed end of the instrument to prick Bear's right leg. It jumped.

"He's a lucky man," he said, tossing back the scalpel. "He'll be able to walk to the gallows."

The sergeant's breath came out in a whoosh. "Good work, Doc! Remind me to talk to you about sending a case of that loudium stuff to Doc Hollander back at Fort Benton."

Wilson ceased bandaging to glare at him. "That's not funny, Sergeant," he said. "Not funny at all."

"How long before he can be moved?" asked Trainer.

"Couple of days. This is twice you've booted me out of my bed, Murdock. This time I hope I get paid."

"I'll settle my bill before I leave town," I assured him. "For the rest, you'll have to talk to the captain. He's his prisoner, not mine."

The captain adjusted his slicker. "If you're not too tired,

Deputy, I'd like to see you in the sheriff's office in a few minutes."

"I'm not paying the bill."

"Your sense of humor wears thin after a while." He strode toward the front of the shop and the exit. "Sergeant, I want a guard posted in front of this building at all times. I'll send someone to spell you in an hour."

The sergeant grumbled something unintelligible, which may or may not have contained the words, "Yes, sir."

I remained behind a few minutes to make sure Bear was resting comfortably, then left to join the captain at the jail. At the door, I almost bumped into a big trooper who was on his way out. I had never seen this one before. He had a coarse face overhung by massive black brows and shoulders like a workhorse; by most standards I suppose he was huge, but I had just spent ten days with the biggest, so I was less than impressed. He brushed past me without a word.

Inside, Henry's coffee pot was sizzling away atop the stove, filling the room with its familiar acrid odor. Henry's rifles and shotgun were locked in the rack where he'd left them. Captain Trainer, still wearing the slicker, was sitting behind Henry's desk smoking one of Henry's cigars and reading one of the wanted circulars Henry had stacked there. A puddle was spreading beneath Trainer's hat where he had dropped it atop the desk.

"Who's the buffalo?" I asked.

"That's Corporal Patterson. He's been filling in as sheriff in my absence. He'll be back after supper. Sit down."

"He looks capable." I dropped into the chair before the desk and tilted my hat forward over my eyes. Moisture seeped from the brim down into my collar; I let it.

"He should be," he said. "He was a sergeant-major before I broke him for striking an officer."

"Anyone I know?"

He let that one slide. I heard the water dripping from his oilskin to the floor.

"We're both exhausted," he began, "so I'll make this short and sweet. Will you agree to testify against Bear Anderson at his trial?"

That sank in slowly. "What do you care one way or the other?" I asked finally. "You won't have anything to do with it once you turn him over to the civil authorities."

"I'm not turning him over to the civil authorities. As soon as he's well enough, he'll be tried in military court-martial."

I straightened my hat and sat up. "Anderson's a civilian. The military has no jurisdiction over him."

He sent a jet of blue smoke toward the darkened ceiling. "It's perfectly legal. Federal law states that the military may intervene in cases where the civil courts have ceased to function. Staghorn has no permanent judge, and the circuit judge can't get in until the passes are cleared. Technically, due process of law has been suspended."

"Nothing in the law says you can't wait until spring."

"Nothing in the law says I have to."

"Whoever heard of a captain presiding over a military court-martial?"

"The circumstances are unique. There will be no peace between the Indians and the settlers while Anderson goes unpunished. Delay on our part will be construed by Two Sisters as official sanction for his actions. And it's not just him. The Blackfeet are getting restless and so are the Crows. The fact that they're no friends of the Flatheads means little as long as a renegade white is allowed to go around killing Indians. If we don't act now, next year's thaw will bring a full-scale war like this territory hasn't seen since the Little Big Horn. A wire to General Clifton should remove most of the legal obstacles that remain."

"You've got it all figured out, haven't you? All that's left is to measure the rope."

"Fifteen feet, I should think, allowing for the knots and Anderson's height and weight."

I showed him my gun. His expression didn't change.

"That's not your style, Murdock. Even if it were, you'd have no place to go afterwards."

"Murder is relative," I told him. But I put the gun away. Instead, I gripped the edges of the desk and leaned forward until our faces were only inches apart. "I'll tell you what is my style. I'm no lawyer, but I've seen my share of them in action in Judge Blackthorne's court. When that court-martial convenes, I'm representing Bear Anderson."

The twisted smile returned. "Suit yourself. The outcome will be the same regardless of what you do or say."

I straightened. "You're the enemy," I said. "Not Bear. Not the Indians. You."

His cigar had gone out. He relit it, lifting the chimney of the lamp on the desk and leaning forward to engage the flame. "That's all for now, Deputy," he said, between puffs. "I suppose we'll meet again in court."

CHAPTER FIFTEEN

He was scheduled to hang shortly after dawn on a bleak day in December.

As expected, the trial had been a joke. Chief witness for the prosecution was old White Mane, whose whiskey-roughened voice shook as he described the aftermath of what was already being whispered about abroad as the Spring Thaw Massacre, and repeated the dying words of its sole survivor. It mattered little that this was pure hearsay, or that a significant number of the details had changed since the first time he had recounted the story to Bart Goddard, or even that every time he opened his mouth the air reeked of the profitable side of Goddard's mercantile. It didn't matter at all that I raised objections remarking upon each of these points. Trainer turned such arguments aside with the grace of a boxer feeling out his opponent—never actually landing a punch, but rendering mine ineffective through simple footwork. The emotion-swaying tricks I'd learned observing the transplanted eastern attorneys in Helena were useless in the stylized atmosphere of a military court-martial. Bear was twisting in the wind before the first bang of the gavel.

Before the trial, I had made several attempts to wire Judge Blackthorne to inform him of Trainer's unorthodox proceedings, only to be turned away each time by armed guards stationed at the door of the telegraph office. The captain, they told me, had declared martial law in view of the "Flathead danger," and put a stop to all messages traveling into and out of town. The restriction was eventually lifted, but by that time high winds had taken down the telegraph lines, thus severing Staghorn's last link with civilization. Trainer couldn't have planned it any better.

But weather is a fickle thing that recognizes no ally.

For two weeks following the passage of sentence, blizzards kept the troopers from carrying it out. Even then, two of the men assigned to construct a gallows behind the jail were killed when a sudden blast of wind from the North tore the supports from beneath them, hurled them to the ground, and brought half a ton of fresh lumber crashing down on top of them. Not counting the Indians we'd slaughtered back at the crossing, that made it nine dead just since I'd renewed my acquaintance with Bear Anderson. Bringing him to task was proving an expensive proposition for whoever tried it.

At length, however, the gallows were built, and beneath a pale sun the citizens of Staghorn gathered in the old firebreak behind the jail, stamping their feet and pounding their shoulders with gloved and mittened fists to keep the circulation moving while they waited for the back door to open. It was an impressive gathering; merchants had closed their shops, and farmers, trappers, and cattlemen had braved the arduous journey to town in order to see history in the making. It wasn't every day you got to see a legend die.

And they were not the only spectators.

Since dawn they had begun to accumulate along the rocky ridge overlooking town, and by the time the jail door opened, the skyline was filled with mounted Indians decked in all their ceremonial finery. For the first time in memory, the Flatheads had not made their regular migration to the plains west of the Bitterroot to await the spring thaw. Two Sisters had chosen to winter in the mountains rather than miss the hanging.

On the gallows itself, backs to the wind, stood Captain Trainer and Corporal Patterson. Patterson was a last-minute substitution for the sergeant, who, upon learning that he was to be the hangman, had gotten drunk and started a brawl that wrecked Goddard's saloon just after the old bastard had finished repairing the damage wrought by Ira Longbow. Trainer had locked him up in the cell adjacent to the scalp-hunter's pending possible court-martial. I saw the sergeant come to the window of his cell from time to time to glance down at the proceedings; from the expression on his face I wondered if he had been as drunk as he'd seemed, or if his one-man riot had been staged to keep him from being the one who sprang the trap.

The local minister—pudgy, bespectacled and mumbling from a Bible held open in his mittened hands—was the first to descend the long flight of wooden steps that led from the back door of the jail to ground level. Behind him walked Bear, bare-headed and in chains, his hands manacled behind his back. A chorus of mingled gasps and murmurs greeted him as he ducked his head and swiveled sideways to get through the doorway; most of those present had never seen him, and to a generation that considered a man over six feet tall to be gigantic, the sight of Anderson's nearly seven feet of gristle was beyond belief. Trailing him were the remaining eleven troopers. The captain wasn't taking any chances here, as the odd man followed at a safe distance with his side arm in hand, while behind him the others marched in a column of twos with their rifles in parade position at their shoulders. There was no drum; the condemned man was a civilian, after all, and some of the conventions had to be honored. So silence reigned.

Fourteen steps led to the scaffold. The extra had been

added as an afterthought to compensate for Bear's great height, even as the strongest rope in town had been sought to support his tremendous weight. He mounted them with ease in spite of the chains that linked his ankles and wrists. His expression was impossible to read.

The first trooper followed him to the top while the others took up a position of attention on the ground in front of the gallows. There, a buckboard with an empty coffin on the back and a teamster with a bad cold waited to transport the body to the cemetery south of town. At intervals the teamster helped himself to a healthy swig from a bottle he had on the seat beside him to relieve his sniffles; the gurgling noise it made as he tipped it up sounded ridiculously loud in the charged atmosphere of the firebreak.

I was standing in the alley between the jail and the deserted dress shop next door, a vantage point the crowd had overlooked, probably because of the icy gusts that whistled unhampered through the narrow gap. From there I had a good view of the scaffold and the Indians on the ridge. I spotted Two Sisters mounted at the northern end of the line, wearing ceremonial feathers and a coat pieced together from the kind of pelts the Flatheads considered too fine to waste in trade with the other nations. His feelings concerning the scene unfolding below him must have been mixed; no doubt he was pleased to see his people's killer punished, but at the same time he was losing the one excuse he needed to unite the northwestern tribes in a war against the whites.

"Any last words?" Trainer asked Bear, as the noose was slipped over his head.

"I come here to die, not make a speech," he said. "Let's ride."

The reply was a disappointment to some of the spectators, who had evidently been hoping to hear something of historical or biblical origin. I saw Jack Dodsworth of the Staghorn *Republican* flip shut his notepad with a disgusted gesture. They couldn't know that those last two words were a summary of Bear's whole life.

There was nothing else to do, but do it. A glance passed between Trainer and the corporal, and at a nod from the captain the noose was drawn tight and a black cloth hood was tugged down over that magnificent leonine head. Patterson stepped away from the trap and stood with his hand on the wooden lever, waiting. Trainer's arm came up, stopped. For a space they might have been puppets on a miniature stage, Goliath and his armorers in a biblical re-enactment, awaiting David's entrance. Then the arm came down. The lever was released with a squeak.

The trap fell, banging at the end of the leather straps that held it. Bear plunged through the opening. The rope jerked taut, stretched—and broke.

The shattered end sprang upward, wrapping itself around the gallows' wooden arm. Bear, still wearing the noose, hit the ground hard and lay kicking in the mud and slush. He was strangling.

I was halfway down to the firebreak when Trainer recovered from his initial shock and ran down the steps, taking them two at a time. By the time he got there, Ezra Wilson, who had been standing by waiting to sign the death certificate, was kneeling beside the body and struggling to loosen the noose with his hands. The officer reached past him and sawed at the rope with his knife. It parted and fell. Wilson tore away the black hood.

"Pierce!" shouted the captain. "Another rope! On the double!"

A trooper left formation and took off at a sprint up the

slope. The others dropped their rifles to hip level and moved forward to drive back the pressing crowd. I slipped past them.

"You tried once," I panted, reaching Trainer. "Isn't that enough?"

He turned his vague gray eyes in my direction, but said nothing.

"Somebody'd better do something, and fast." Wilson was straining every muscle to hold down Bear's heaving shoulders. "His neck is broken."

"Hurry up with that rope!" the captain roared.

The trooper returned a moment later bearing a coil of rope, and he and Patterson secured one end and slung the other over the gallows arm. While a noose was being fashioned, Trainer, another trooper, and I lifted Bear to his feet and hustled him up the steps. If I couldn't help him any other way, I could at least help him die.

This time Patterson didn't bother with the hood and he didn't wait for the order to drop the trap. As soon as the noose was in place he tripped the lever.

This time the rope held. The gallows creaked, the scaffold swayed; for a moment it seemed as if the entire structure might collapse. Bear kicked twice and dangled.

A gust of wind caught the gallows arm and twisted it around, straining still further the nails and pegs that held the structure together. Then it died. The great body swung in silence.

The minister remembered his job suddenly and began reading from the Book of Genesis.

I think it was that first failure on the part of the hangman that led to the rumor, which persists, that Bear Anderson survived that day, and that someone else was hanged in his stead. It doesn't seem to matter that any attempt to

sneak him out would have had to have taken place in front
of more than a hundred witnesses, not counting the Indians, and that nobody but a perfect double could have
taken his place the second time, as that time he was
hanged without the hood over his head. Legends don't per-
ish that easily. As late as last year he was seen in St. Louis
driving a trolley, and there's no indication that these sight-
ings will cease until time makes his further survival impossible.

I do nothing to discourage such talk. Although I stopped
carrying a badge six years ago, when Judge Blackthorne
died and they brought in an assistant district attorney from
New Hampshire to replace him, people still seek me out on
occasion to ask about Bear and the time we rode together
up in the Bitterroot. When the conversation approaches
the hanging, I change the subject. They'd resent me if I
tried to force the truth down their throats, and in any case
they wouldn't believe me. It's easier among the Indians,
where there is no written history and the storytellers can
leave out the last part in order to keep the myth going.
Now that Two Sisters and most of the braves who were
there that day are gone, and the Flatheads themselves are
socked away on reservations, it's an easy thing for them to
believe that Mountain That Walks still prowls those rocks
on the back of his big dun horse, his belt a tangle of bloody
scalps, looking for fresh victims. He's become part of their
heritage, and when the bad feelings are done between red
and white, and scholars begin collecting these stories and
putting them down on paper, you can bet that Bear will be
there in some form. That's when he'll prove to be as inde-
structible as the legends say.

On that day, however, there was no doubt. When it was
certain that the rope had done its job, Captain Trainer

undid the knot that anchored it and allowed the body to fall of its own weight to the ground. Wilson bent over it, pried open each eyelid, and straightened.

"He's dead."

The statement carried up to the ridge, and after a few minutes Chief Two Sisters wheeled his horse and led his braves back into the shelter of the high rocks.

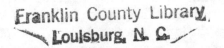